UNCLE PAUL

CELIA FREMLIN

UNCLE PAUL

faber

First published in 1959 by Gollancz
This edition first published in 2023
by Faber & Faber Ltd
The Bindery
51 Hatton Garden
London EC1N 8HN

Typeset by Typo•glyphix, Burton-on-Trent DE14 3HE
Printed and bound in the UK by CPI Group (UK) Ltd, Croydon CR0 4YY

A CIP record for this book
is available from the British Library

ISBN 978–0–571–38087–9

Printed and bound in the UK on FSC® certified paper in line with our continuing
commitment to ethical business practices, sustainability and the environment.
For further information see faber.co.uk/environmental-policy

4 6 8 10 9 7 5 3

To Elia

CHAPTER I

It is rare for any catastrophe to seem like a catastrophe right at the very beginning. Nearly always, in its early stages, it seems more like a nuisance; just one more of those tiresome interruptions which come so provokingly just when life is going smoothly and pleasantly.

Looking back afterwards, Meg could never be sure whether she had felt like this about Isabel's telegram. For memory is a deceptive thing. It was so easy, later, when fear had grown into certainty, to imagine that she had had a premonition of it all. That she had known, all through that rainy summer day, as the typewriters clicked and pinged, as the top copies and the file copies piled up under the watery light, that when she got back to her lodgings there would be a message like this awaiting her. That a telegram would be stuck corner-wise in the letter rack just inside the great gloomy front door; that it would be from Isabel; and that, this time, the trouble would be real.

Or had the whole thing, after all, only seemed like a nuisance? When she saw who the telegram was from, even when she read the message, had she still merely thought, with exasperated affection, that this was just another of Isabel's *things*—a fuss about nothing? For Isabel *was* a worrier, always had been; and since marrying for the second time, setting up house all over again with a stepfather for her two little boys, she had seemed worse than ever. There was a tenseness about her now; a puckered, flustered look about her small, anxious mouth that Meg had not seen there before.

Well, no, that wasn't quite true. Meg *had* seen it before, of course, even in their nursery days. A sister can never really show you a new expression on her face. It is just that expressions which once came only in occasional unhappy flashes may become more frequent—habitual; while other expressions, once habitual, may now only flash out occasionally, in moments of lightness and snatched gaiety.

High up in the grey London apartment house, Meg looked at the telegram again. In the past minutes it had become familiar to her, part of her environment. The very folds and creases it had acquired from its journey in and out of her pocket seemed to make it, uncomfortably, more and more a part of her, less and less easy to gloss over or ignore.

"Mildred needs help. Please come.

Isabel."

Meg knew already that she would go. Even if it *was* only one of Isabel's ridiculous flaps, she would still go. She had always gone when Isabel was in any kind of trouble, particularly if the trouble concerned Mildred. Mildred was something that she and Isabel had to cope with together; it had always been like that, even in the days when they were children, and it was Mildred who was supposed to be coping with them . . .

But Meg did not want to think about her childhood just now. Such thoughts would lead, inevitably, to that bit of her childhood which mustn't be spoken of in front of Mildred. Even after all these years, a reminder of those weeks could still throw Mildred into such a state of hysterical self-pity as might take days to soothe. In dealing with Mildred's problems it was better not even to think about that time. Better, always, to think only of what to *do*—of the practical details.

Such as looking up the trains to—where was it?—Southcliffe—this place where Isabel and Philip had taken the children for their holiday. Perhaps, Meg mused, as she scanned the columns of tiny, tightly packed figures, perhaps this holiday would be doing Isabel good—would be softening her mouth again, smoothing out the tiny, fluttering creases between her brows. Though how much of a holiday it could be for her, staying in a caravan with two little boys and an exacting and by no means youthful husband who still wasn't really used to the children . . .

Southcliffe. Only a two-hour journey, apparently. She could go down after work tomorrow—even get away at lunch time, perhaps—and, if it turned out that nothing much was the matter, she could be back on Sunday in time to go out with Freddy as arranged.

But, of course, she must ring Freddy, just to warn him that she might not be there, and not to wait for her if she didn't turn up. Not that he would be likely to wait for her in any case. Freddy didn't seem the kind of man who would wait for anybody. Or was there, perhaps, some kind of a

girl, quite different from Meg, for whom he *would* wait—
for whom he might even arrive punctually himself—?

Well, anyway, it would only be polite to ring him. And
perhaps, having got him to the telephone, she might consult
him about the whole business. Tell him about Isabel, about
Mildred. Ask his advice about going to Southcliffe.

Meg stared out over the rooftops at the rainy summer
twilight, and thought about consulting Freddy. About
dialling his number, and then waiting the long seconds
while he slid languidly off his divan and strolled across the
room to the telephone; and then she would hear his voice,
his soft, deceptively intimate voice, saying something
aggravating.

Or perhaps not answering at all. It must be nearly nine
already. No time, now, for weighing up the subtle balance
of pleasure and embarrassment involved in such a call. Meg
hunted four pennies from the bottom of her bag and ran
down the long flights of stairs to the telephone in the hall.

"Oh—Freddy! So you *are* still there. Listen. It's about
Sunday. And I want your advice about something, it's
very—What? Oh! I'm sorry—this is Meg, I mean—"

How he always managed to make one look silly!—and
then, a second later, warmed one into utter forgiveness!
Already the slow, mellow enticement—none the less fascinating for being almost certainly bogus—was back in his
voice, and she could tell that the half mocking, half affec-
tionate smile was beginning to flicker round his mouth. She
could tell, too, that his long, musician's fingers were at this
moment coiling themselves round the receiver in the only,

4

in the most perfectly comfortable position. Other people grabbed up receivers just anyhow.

"Oh, I see. My advice." Freddy's voice, without the faintest trace of an accent, had yet somehow a faintly un-English quality that Meg could not define. "You mean," he went on, brightening, "that you are going to tell me of some decision you have reached, and to order me to agree with it. But of course, my sweet. It'll be a pleasure. I agree with it absolutely and entirely. We don't need to go through all the wearisome formality of you telling me what it's all about and me listening, do we?" he added anxiously.

"Oh, *Freddy*! Stop it!" Meg was half laughing, half piqued. "Something's happened. Really. At least, I think so. And I really *do* want your advice."

There was a little pause at the other end of the line. Meg seemed to see him shifting his position, hunching his shoulder yet more luxuriously against the instrument.

"My advice? But why *mine*, darling? I mean to say, there couldn't *be* a worse person than myself to advise a young girl living alone in the big city. My advice is usually immoral and always impractical. Anyone'll tell you."

"Yes—but Freddy—Oh *please* stop being like that for a minute, and listen. You see, it's the family. Isabel says—"

"Quarrel with them," came the instructions down the wire, decisively. "It's the only way with families. Quarrel with them *now*, while you're still young. If you leave it till you're older, you'll find that you owe them all so much money that you can't afford to. So quarrel, girl, quarrel for your life! And then come round and have a drink. In about half an hour."

5

The telephone clicked into silence, and Meg turned away, laughing, and knowing that she should be annoyed. It ought to be humiliating to be so taken for granted by a man whom she had known for so short a time; but it wasn't humiliating at all; it was fun; and when, a few minutes later, she stuffed the telegram into her handbag to show to Freddy, it seemed more like a ticket for some long-anticipated theatre performance than a disquieting piece of news.

The interminable wet length of summer daylight was still stretching through the almost deserted streets when Meg reached Freddy's block of flats. Freddy, like herself, lived on a top floor, but here there was a porter, and a lift, and Meg was soon hurrying along the corridor towards Freddy's door, from behind which a piano could be heard pouring forth notes with astonishing speed and exuberance, and also with astonishing disregard (astonishing, that is, to anyone unacquainted with Freddy) of the inhabitants of the adjoining flats.

"You're wet!"

Freddy, clad in a scarlet silk dressing gown, had flung open his door in a gesture of exaggerated welcome, and was now drawing back a pace in somewhat unreasonable dismay.

"*And* you're wearing a raincoat!" he continued, even more unreasonably. "Here I stand, my heart going pit-a-pat, my arms outstretched, waiting for my lady love, and when she arrives she's wet. And wearing a *raincoat*!"

Suddenly he grinned, an impish grin that lit his rather sallow, triangular face to extraordinary brilliancy, and seizing Meg's arm he pulled her into his sitting-room and switched on the electric fire.

"There! Now you can take that thing off! And first, before you tell me the long sad story of your life, tell me why you haven't come here in a beautiful dress that sweeps the floor? And high heels? And something sparkling in your hair?"

Meg glanced down thoughtfully at her brogues.

"Well—it's raining," she observed. "I mean, it would be silly to dress up to walk all this way in the rain. You'd just look a mess at the end of it."

Freddy shook his head sadly.

"What an outlook! What an attitude to life! When skies are grey, my dear—didn't any of your aunts ever tell you that one? No, I suppose not; aunts aren't like that any more, they all go out to work. But now—let me see—" Pulling the raincoat from Meg's shoulders, he stepped back and surveyed her, head on one side, with the air of a connoisseur. "I want to see you as my Ideal Woman for a moment. Green and silver, I fancy—very full in the skirt and very tight in the bodice, with perhaps a touch of lace just *here*. And silver shoes—no, sandals—very high heels, of course. And the hair piled high—great masses of it—a sort of Edwardian style—"

Suddenly bunching up her light brown curls between his hands, he turned her face towards the mirror. "See? It suits you. Really. Have it done that way."

For a moment Meg caught a glimpse of her own flushed, excited face in the mirror, before it stiffened into self-consciousness under her own scrutiny. Hastily she shook herself free, laughing, but a trifle brusque.

"No," she said. "No, I don't think so. It would be an awful bother to look after. And it wouldn't look like *me*."

Freddy sighed.

"Well—there—I never said it would," he agreed amicably. "I only said it would look like my Ideal Woman. Well, never mind. Let's hear about the family skeleton, since that's what you've come for. If we can't talk about ideal women—why, then, we'll talk about skeletons. Of course. Why not? Do you keep it in your handbag?" he added with interest, as Meg proceeded to fumble for Isabel's telegram.

"Here," she said, extracting the envelope. "Read it, and I'll explain . . ."

The explanation took a long time. At the end of it Freddy, with the air of a schoolboy going over his history homework, leaned earnestly towards her.

"Let me see," he began. "Just check that I'm getting it right, will you? Mildred is your half-sister, twenty years older than you are, and she managed your father's house and looked after you like a mother. Or, anyway, like an aunt. Or—" holding up his hand to forestall Meg's interruption—"or like a French governess. Anyway, she went through the motions of bringing you up after your mother's death. Right? And Isabel is your own sister, a few years older than yourself, only far less competent—no, don't interrupt me, please. Both these sisters of yours are, in their different ways, contrary, self-centred sort of creatures—'Highly strung' was, I believe, the euphemism that their long-suffering little sister has just applied to them—and they have both formed the touching habit of expecting her—the

8

little sister—to help them out of any jams they choose to muddle themselves into. And really, you know, this habit doesn't surprise me. For poor little Cinderella, in this case, is clever as well as angelic. She can manage other people's affairs much more competently than they can themselves, and so naturally the two wicked step-sisters—"

"Oh, Freddy, they *aren't*!" protested Meg. "They aren't my step-sisters at all. I've explained to you. Mildred's my half-sister—my father was *her* father too—and Isabel—"

"Spare me the family tree all over again!" cried Freddy, with an air of exaggerated suffering. "Trying to make out who is related to who in families where someone has married twice gives me pins and needles. Really it does. It's a sort of complex. They made me learn about the Wars of the Roses when I was too young, I think. Besides," he continued, returning to the attack. "Your sister's done it too, hasn't she? Married twice, I mean."

"Isabel? Oh, yes, she has, of course, but—"

"And Mildred? The redoubtable Mildred, who manages so cunningly to keep you all dancing attendance? Has *she* any other husbands to her name? Or is there only the elderly and evanescent Hubert, whose recurrent absences from home you have been so graphically describing?"

"No—I mean, I didn't really say that Hubert—That is—"

Meg stopped. Had she been giving away too much already of Mildred's private affairs? Giving them away to a comparative stranger—a man whom she had met for the first time barely a month ago? Not that Mildred herself was particularly reticent about her problems. Indeed, she would sometimes hold forth about her wrongs in the most surprisingly assorted company, retailing, with apparent gusto, intimate grievances and slights that most women would have preferred to keep hidden. But there were other times, too, when she could be excessively touchy at any reference to her troubles, even if (or, Meg sometimes fancied, particularly if) it took the form of an offer of help. Mildred had always been perverse and difficult; had she been growing more so of late?

"But what good," Freddy was saying, judicially, "do you think *you* can do by getting involved in it all? It sounds to me as if there's a family row going on, and you're well out of it. Particularly if, as you say, they've only got a four-berth caravan to have it in. Whoever's side you take by day, you'll also have to take their blankets by night. You'll be a mixed blessing, my dear. *Very* mixed."

Meg shook her head.

"My family don't have rows, exactly," she said. "They get into *states*, and then somebody's got to do something. I mean, if Hubert's left Mildred again, and Mildred's gone dashing down to the caravan because she can't bear to be alone at the flat—and of course there won't be room for her at the caravan, so they'll have to find a hotel for her, and the hotels'll all be full up at this time of year, and Philip will be furious, because he can't stand Mildred in any case, even when he isn't being expected to chase round finding a room for her, and that'll make Isabel go sort of helpless the way she does when Philip's in a temper—"

"My dear child! Listen to yourself! Just listen! It terrifies me. Really it does. If you let yourself talk like that, you'll soon find yourself living like that, too. Your whole life will become a rigmarole like the one you have just recited—and with the same lack of punctuation and main verbs. I'm warning you. I'm warning you *now*. Keep out of it. Let them get on with it. I'll take you for a drive at the weekend instead. A hundred miles each way—with punctuation *and* main verbs. There. I can't say fairer than that."

Meg shook her head.

"No, Freddy. Really. I've got to go. Isabel wouldn't have sent the telegram if it wasn't important. At least, it mightn't seem important to outsiders, but—"

Freddy suddenly switched his ground, and grinned at her provokingly.

"I'm beginning to feel that I'd like to meet these two selfish sisters of yours," he declared. "I've always felt like that, you know, about the Cinderella story. We have Cinderella, so sweet, so obliging, so beautiful—why, naturally she gets the prince. Why shouldn't she? It's dull. It's obvious. It's like water running down a drain pipe—it couldn't go any other way. But the Ugly Sisters—Ah, that's the challenge! Ugly, selfish, thoroughly dislikeable—yet they still *almost* get the prince. They come within a hair's breadth of it. *That* was the achievement; *that* was the real core of the story. A glorious failure, beside which Cinderella's success is limp and insipid. Don't you think so?"

But Meg was looking at the clock.

"It's nearly eleven!" she cried, jumping up with an appearance of greater dismay than she really felt in order to cover up her inability to think of any witty and appropriate response to all this. "I must go at once, or I may not be able to get in, and then I'll have to knock someone up, and——"

"And lose your reputation, all for nothing," finished Freddy, nodding his head sympathetically. "I quite see your point. Never mind. Sure you wouldn't like to stay a little longer and hear some more of my new and original interpretations of the well-known fairy tales? No? I could do Bluebeard for you, if you like," he added invitingly.

"No——no, thank you! Another time." Meg hastily and rather ungracefully huddled herself into her coat, and stuffed her handbag under her arm. "Another time, when I feel more like Bluebeard's wife." Did that sound witty? Sophisticated? As if she knew what he was talking about? "And I might——if I'm back that is——I'll be seeing you on Sunday?"

He grinned enigmatically.

"*Did* Cinderella see the prince on Sunday? After she'd polished off the ugly sisters. I don't remember. I must look it up for you. Yes, I'll certainly look it up and let you know——in answer to the postcard you are going to send me with your address, and your window marked with a cross. I'm sorry, your caravan chimney. Or your tent pole. Or the spot where they arrested you for vagrancy when it turned out that there was no room for you in the caravan, just as I said. Goodbye, my sweet; and don't say you weren't warned."

CHAPTER II

The washing lines strung between the caravans were all sagging, but Isabel's sagged more than most. Meg felt that she would have recognised her sister's caravan at once, even without the detailed and painstaking directions that had arrived this morning, following on the telegram. It was the most lop-sided one; the one adjoining the expanse of dusty stinging-nettles that is to be found somewhere on every caravan site; and its door was warped so that it either couldn't be opened or else couldn't be shut.

This was one of the occasions when it couldn't be opened, and as Meg set down her suitcase in order to struggle with it more efficiently, she began to feel annoyed. Probably the Calor gas stove would turn out to be the only one on the site that wasn't working, and one of the bunks would keep coming off its hinges.

Not that any of this would be poor Isabel's fault. She must have rented the caravan by letter, and it was the owner's responsibility to see to this sort of thing, not hers. All the same, why did Isabel's arrangements *always* have to turn out like this? Why did Isabel herself always have to be—well— so Isabel-ish? Meg felt, confusedly, that Isabel ought to have changed more. Surely, when she marries a new husband, a woman should become, in some way, different? Should wear different clothes—read different books—something.

Should at least go away for a different sort of holiday. Glancing round at the worn, untidy grass, Meg felt that though this seaside place might have a different name from the others, it was really the same. Too much the same. Was Isabel becoming one of those women with the devastating knack of carrying sameness about with them, like a suitcase, all over the world?

"You have to bash it, sort of."

Meg looked round in some relief.

"Hullo, Johnnie! Haven't you grown!"

Like most young and inexperienced aunts, Meg had resolved at the outset never to make this idiotic remark to any of her nephews or nieces. But, when it came to the point, it was beyond one's control. After a few months' absence this was, so overwhelmingly, the first thing one noticed about a child. A swollen, outsize sort of look—a new ring in the voice—an unfamiliarity. As always, it only lasted a moment; already he had shrunk to just Johnnie again, exactly the same, even to the piece of grey sticking plaster peeling off his knee.

"You have to bash it—like this."

With the unnerving skill and assurance of the expert, Johnnie hurled himself side on against the door, which burst open, revealing immediately Isabel's beach bag, knitting, library book and mackintosh, all piled together on the seat of a canvas chair.

Well, at least it's probably not the same library book, Meg reflected, and turned to pick up her suitcase. Half way up the steps she stopped, undecided.

"Johnnie," she said. "Do you know if I'm supposed to be staying actually *in* the caravan? Will there be room, I mean? Did your mother say anything about it? And where is she? Am I early?"

Out of this list, Johnnie expertly selected the question he deemed worthy of an answer.

"No," he said. "You're just in time for the bathe. I'm not allowed to without a grown up." Grabbing off the floor of the caravan a sandy shred of navy blue worsted, twisted, as children's bathing-suits always are, into a tight figure-of-eight, he waved it towards Meg in an encouraging half-circle that flipped damp sand in every direction. "Come on."

"No, Johnnie, wait!" Meg protested, laughing and brushing the sand off her skirt. "I can't just rush into the sea with you like that. I haven't unpacked yet—and I don't even know where I'm supposed to be staying. Where's your mother? On the beach?" She looked this way and that among the crowded ranks of caravans. It was hard to guess, here, even the direction of the sea.

"What?" said Johnnie. But he noticed, now, that Meg had a suitcase in her hand. Grown ups with suitcases, he had already observed, accurately but incuriously, always went on like this.

"I suppose I can't bathe, then," he summed up gloomily. He hadn't listened to his aunt's last speech, but this, he was sure, was what it all amounted to. "And they won't let me bathe after tea, either. I'll have to play cricket with Daddy."

Meg could not help laughing.

"Don't you like playing cricket?" she asked, but even this seemed, at the moment, to be beyond the range of Johnnie's one-track mind.

"I was going to bathe with the bungalow lot," he went on doggedly, "but they've gone out in a car, or something. And then Mummy said *she'd* be back in time to bathe with me, but she isn't, and—"

"Back-from-where?" Meg condensed the words almost into a single syllable hoping that, if she was quick enough, she might be able to snatch some useful information from her nephew before his thoughts had proceeded further on their relentless course. It was like trying to jump on to a moving train.

"From Aunt Mildred's," said Johnnie; and Meg had the sensation of dropping into the corner seat, breathless and triumphant. "She went straight there after dinner," Johnnie continued obligingly, "because Aunt Mildred was crying, or something. That's why we couldn't bathe—"

With juggler's speed, Meg retrieved the conversation:

"Where is Aunt Mildred. Staying in the town, or what?"

"She seemed to be just crying," said Johnnie, detachedly; and before this rather unhelpful contribution as to his aunt's whereabouts could be further elucidated, his face suddenly lit up.

"There's Mummy!" he squealed; and, bathing-suit in hand, he streaked across the dry, yellowing grass towards the wire fence and the dusty white path along which Meg herself had approached the encampment.

Isabel was looking tired and strained. Her print dress was a shade too long, and she carried a limp canvas shopping bag. Isabel always carried a shopping bag, wherever she went. For years Meg had meant to ask her why such a bag was so invariably needed, but it never seemed quite the right moment. Nor was it the right moment now: Isabel had caught sight of her sister, and her face had suddenly brightened and softened unbelievably with an upsurge of the old childhood affection.

'Oh, Meg, how lovely to see you! Oh, I am glad! Oh, it'll be so much easier now!"

But even as she linked arms with her sister, Isabel's features were falling once more into the familiar anxious lines: "No, Johnnie, I can't. I've told you I can't. I've got to collect Peter from the Hutchinses. I'm late already, I said I'd fetch him before tea, and I don't know what time they have their tea, I expect it's earlier than us. And I've got to see about the beds, too, and the water takes such a long time to heat on that stove. I'm sure there's something wrong with the supply—"

Of course, Johnnie wasn't listening. He knew that people often used a tremendous number of words to say "No"—or even "Yes," for that matter—and he didn't really mind. He only had to wait until the flow of speech ended, and then he could ask again.

But Meg was listening. And watching, too, unhappily, as the worried expressions flitted back and forth across her sister's face. Was Isabel really upset? And, if so, was it about Mildred, about some big, important trouble, or was it merely about these tiny domestic difficulties that she always allowed to loom so large? And if it *was* only these trifles—if she could look like that and feel like that about such things—wasn't that the biggest, most important trouble of all? To be a person so easily weighed down—so little able to enjoy her life?

Meg checked herself. It wasn't fair to criticise Isabel like this, when she didn't even know yet what was the matter. Johnnie had said that Aunt Mildred was crying—not that that was anything new, but you could never tell. It is easy to forget that people who cry about trifles may also cry about disasters. She turned again to Isabel:

"Mildred?" she asked. "How is she?"

Meg spoke in a low voice in deference to Johnnie's restless presence—in deference, rather, to the accepted conventions about conversations in the presence of children. For she could not but feel that the precaution was, in Johnnie's case, superfluous. The seagulls themselves could scarcely have been attending less, swooping hither and thither, shrilly, self-centredly whining after their own affairs.

"I've just been seeing her," answered Isabel, also in a dutiful undertone. "Oh, Meg, it's such a *nuisance*!" The words burst forth spontaneously, with piercing sincerity, and Isabel immediately apologised for them: "I don't mean that—I mean it's dreadful for Mildred, of course, I'm terribly sorry for her. I've been up there all the afternoon."

"Has Hubert left her again?"

"Yes. No. That is, I think he's still at the flat. She's left *him* this time, you might say. But that isn't it, Meg. She's not just upset this time. She's frightened. Really frightened.

18

And Philip says it's all nonsense, and not to humour her. He's *furious* about it. He's trying to get hold of Hubert. He says he must fetch her back. He says it's his job, not ours, and of course it is in a way, but you see Philip doesn't really understand about Mildred. He can't tell when she's just being silly, and when—well—when it's something like this. Oh, Meg!"—Isabel abruptly reversed her whole argument—"Can *you* persuade her that she's just being silly? She'll listen to you more than to any of us. That's partly why I sent for you. Can you convince her that it's all nonsense? Because if not"—Isabel's voice sank lower—"If not, someone'll have to go to the police."

"Someone." It was typical of Isabel to keep the essential, the point of action, as colourless and as indefinite as possible. "I must go." "You must go." "Philip must go"— any of these would have brought to her harassed mind too great a sense of personal involvement, too thick a tangle of adjustments and arrangements, obligations and counter-obligations.

Meg could feel that her sister's thoughts were on the point of trailing off down some anxious by-path of their own, so she hastily recalled them.

"But, Isabel, you haven't told me. What's it all about? What is she frightened of? Not Hubert, surely?"

"No. Oh, no. Not Hubert. At least—"

Meg noticed now that her sister's glance was darting this way and that along the lanes between the caravans; and her arm, still crooked into Meg's own, had stiffened slightly.

"I'll tell you later," she muttered. "I have to fetch Peter back now. The Hutchinses will be thinking—I mean, we were late last time when they had him for me. We'd been to the museum, you see, and I didn't like to make Philip hurry away, he'd think I was making a fuss—Oh, it's all so difficult! Oh dear, and there's Mrs Hutchins at the door! She must have been watching out for me . . ."

Clearly, it wasn't possible to continue the conversation any more just now. Nor did it seem to be possible after they had reached the caravan once more. The moment they got inside, Isabel applied herself to cutting up carrots with a blunt knife, meanwhile casting frequent anxious glances at the clock—one of the few pieces of Isabel's equipment which was (regrettably, Meg felt) in full working order. Quite what the hurry was she could not make out, but she set herself to helping Isabel as best she could. She despatched Johnnie, with a large earthenware jug, to fetch water from the tap; she provided Peter with a piece of string and a bent stick with which to catch sharks in the withered grass under the caravan steps; and then she volunteered to scrape the potatoes.

But Isabel was a difficult person to help—the people most in need of help often are, Meg reflected. She was herself, Isabel explained, using the only basin for the carrots. And there wasn't anywhere for Meg to sit. And to get at the potatoes at all, she (Isabel) would have to fold the table back, and that would mean moving the basin off it, and the carrots, and the colander, and the dirty mugs, and the thermos flask . . .

"It's got broken."

Johnnie displayed the four earthenware pieces in a detached sort of way, as if they were objects of interest that he had happened to come upon outside. A sharp frown creased Isabel's brows, and Meg hastened to the child's defence:

"It's my fault, Isabel—I sent him with it; he was only trying to help——" she began; and then realised that her intervention was quite superfluous. Isabel's frown had not been for Johnnie at all. With extraordinary haste, and without a word of reprimand, she seized the fragments from the child's hands, and, half stumbling down the steps, she ran and stuffed the broken pieces into the bin at the side of the caravan, pushing them well down among the rest of the rubbish and covering them with a piece of news-paper. Then, with a look of quite disproportionate relief, she wedged the lid back on to the bin. Turning round, she met Meg's look of mingled surprise and amusement. Isabel smiled then, sheepishly.

"I know—it does look silly," she said. "You see, it's just that I'm so *thankful* he should have done it before Philip gets back. You see, Philip doesn't always remember that he's only seven; and then, of course, he's spent most of his life in the army—Philip, I mean—and children *do* take a lot of getting used to, I suppose, if they're not your own . . ."

It seemed to Meg that Isabel was explaining a little too hard; that there was something uneasy about her manner as she sidled back up the steps, not quite meeting her sister's eyes. Was Isabel hiding something from her—evading some issue which lay, unknown to Meg, between them? For it did seem odd that, having sent that urgent telegram, she had still not managed to make an opportunity to tell Meg properly about the trouble. All this hurrying, this frantic scraping of carrots—was Isabel deliberately—or, more likely, being Isabel, half-deliberately—playing for time? Time to collect her thoughts? Time to decide how much of the truth to reveal? Or time for something to happen—for someone to make some move—that would take the decision out of her hands?

"Telegram, lady."

Isabel whirled round with such violence that Meg, crouching down to retrieve Peter's string for him from underneath the steps, was almost thrown off her balance. Even before she had righted herself, and got to her feet, her sister had ripped open the envelope, and a look of relief had already replaced the expression that had flashed into her face—an expression that had come and gone so swiftly that Meg could not give a name to it.

"It's from Philip," she said now, her voice warm and natural, Meg thought, for the first time this afternoon. "He can't get back tonight after all, he's going to stay in town. So you can be in the caravan, Meg, for tonight, anyway. Come on; let's leave the silly old stew, and I'll tell you all about everything."

"Silly old stew." After all the frenzied vegetable-chopping and clock-watching that had been rendered up on its behalf, it was heart-warming to hear the thing thus described. Quite absurdly cheered by the phrase, Meg followed her sister into the untidy recesses of the caravan. The hinge of the bunk *had* come away from the wall, but a carefully adjusted biscuit tin had nevertheless rendered the contraption fairly secure. With a grey army blanket folded across it, it made a comfortable enough seat for the two sisters, out of range of the shrill demands of the little boys and the inquisitive eyes of the over-near neighbours.

CHAPTER III

"It all began," said Isabel, "with Mildred and Hubert having another row. She rang me up about it, actually, at the time, but I'm afraid I didn't pay very much attention. I was busy, you see, getting ready to come away, and so as soon as I found that she wasn't hoping to come and stay with us—well, I'm afraid I didn't bother any more about it. I suppose I should have, but honestly, Meg, this sort of thing is *always* happening to Mildred, you can't keep *on* worrying about it, can you? Well, I did ask her what she was going to do—carefully, you know, so she wouldn't think I was inviting her to our place—people do think that sort of thing so easily, don't they, if you sound at all sympathetic. And I *couldn't* have her, could I, now? I mean, with Philip not liking her, and us just going away on holiday—you *do* see, don't you, Meg?"

Foreseeing that the whole story might be side-tracked indefinitely by this mounting barrier of Isabel's self-reproach, Meg hastened to reassure her sister.

"So what did she say she was going to do?" she prompted.

"Well—that was just the bit that I wasn't bothering about," Isabel explained remorsefully. "I could kick myself now, looking back, because if only I'd listened . . . Well, anyway, roughly what she said was that she wanted to go somewhere where she could be alone: quite alone, because nobody understood her—you know, all the usual thing. She said—and this is the part I wish I'd listened to more carefully—she said she was renting a tiny cottage on the coast, miles from anywhere, and absolutely primitive. She wanted to be alone with Nature, she said—"

At this point Meg burst out laughing. The thought of Mildred, with her high heels, her lacquered hair-do, and her armoury of creams and lotions, existing for so much as an hour in the conditions described seemed too absurd. But Isabel silenced her sister with a reproachful glance.

"Yes, that's what *I* thought," she retorted to Meg's unspoken comment. "When she told me about this cottage miles from anywhere I thought, as you do, that she wouldn't stick it for a moment. But she has. She's been there three days. And the anywhere it's miles from"—Isabel lowered her voice portentously—"is *here*! Two and three-quarter miles, actually," she finished, with anxious bathos.

"Oh." Meg felt that she could now finish the story herself, and was relieved that it was no worse. "Oh, I see. And now she's finding it's full of earwigs, and no hot water, and she can't go back to Hubert yet because a woman has her pride. And all the hotels are full up, and so she wants you to do something about it. Is that it?"

"No." Isabel's face was sombre. "I haven't told you everything yet, Meg. I haven't told you about the cottage. Meg, it's *the* cottage!"

For a moment Meg was quite at a loss. Isabel's words meant nothing to her.

"*The* cottage?" she repeated stupidly.

"Oh, Meg, surely you remember? You *must* remember. I know you were very little at the time, but—Meg—you surely remember about—about Uncle Paul?"

There was a short silence; but it was no longer the silence of incomprehension. Sitting there in the hot, dusty clutter of the caravan, both sisters had felt the sudden, ruthless pull of childhood memory. Each of them simultaneously seemed to be sliding back down the years; sliding, slithering, skidding back along the paths of their separate lives, until they landed, together, on the kitchen stairs of the old home. Wide-eyed with fright and a queer excitement, they were leaning over the banisters, listening: two little girls straining their ears, their very souls, in the effort to hear through that closed door some word, some sound, that would explain why Uncle Paul (as they called him) with his dark, insolent eyes, with his gay, enchanting smile, should be going out of their lives, suddenly and for ever.

Isabel stirred, moved uneasily on the hard wooden edge of the bunk.

"*The* cottage," she repeated once more; and this time she knew that Meg would understand. "The cottage where Mildred and Paul were staying for that fortnight just before . . . before . . ."

"I know." Meg hastened to rescue her sister from the morass of evasive reminiscence into which she was about to flounder. "But, Isabel, *why*? I mean, why should Mildred go there of all places? Surely she doesn't want to remind herself all over again—remind everybody—that *she* was

26

the girl in the case? Out of all the cottages in England, why should she choose *that* one?"

Isabel shook her head helplessly.

"I don't think she did choose it, Meg. I'm sure she didn't. I think it's just one of these horrible, extraordinary coincidences. I think Hubert's secretary must have booked it for her—you know how Mildred hates anything like business, she always gets Miss Wynne to do anything like that for her if she can. She must have just told Miss Wynne to find her a tiny cottage in some deserted spot by the sea, and by some awful, one-in-a-million chance, the girl landed on this one."

"A one in *two* million chance I make it," interposed Meg sceptically. "I mean, it's another frantic coincidence that it should be just near where *you* were going for your holiday."

"Oh, no. I can understand that," said Isabel immediately. "After all, everyone knew we were coming here, we arranged it ages ago; and I daresay Miss Wynne thought it would be a good idea to plant Mildred somewhere near us so that we'd have to look after her—pushing the responsibility on to us, sort of thing. And the reason why we've come here is because I vaguely remember it from when we were children. You wouldn't remember, Meg, but this is where we always used to come before Mother died. I daresay that's how Mildred and Paul came to hear of the cottage in the first place. So perhaps none of it is a coincidence, really," she concluded, with the tentative optimism of the non-mathematical pupil who nevertheless knows when a sum *looks* right.

"Yes, I see." Meg thought it over. Put like this, the coincidence did seem less glaring.

"But what are we supposed to do?" she asked. "I mean, what does Mildred say she wants? I can understand her being upset at finding it's the very same cottage, but why can't she just come away? Find another cottage, if she's so set on the simple life. Though why Mildred, of all people—"

"That's just it," interrupted Isabel. "She won't leave. You know how obstinate she can get sometimes, for no reason at all. At least, she kept saying she wouldn't leave when Philip talked to her before. But I think she might, now, if we could only think of anywhere else for her to go. You see, since then, she's had a fright."

"What sort of a fright?" Meg was not sure whether to feel anxious or amused. There were so many things about a lonely cottage that might frighten a lifelong town-dweller like Mildred. The wind howling down the old wide fire-place. The tiny feet of birds tap-tapping in the eaves. A cow snorting outside the window.

"It must have been the night before last," Isabel was saying. "It was about midnight, she told me, and she was lying there, trying to go to sleep, and listening to the owls and the bats outside—that's what she says, but I don't believe anybody can hear bats really, not from indoors, anyway. Isn't their voice too high-pitched, or something? Well, anyway, there she was, lying awake—she'd just taken a couple of sleeping tablets, she told me, but they hadn't done any good—and as she lay there, she heard footsteps. Outside. They came along the track to the cottage, but they didn't go past. They stopped. And then, she says, after a minute, she heard them again. Sort of scuffling about round the back door. And then, after a bit, they went away again, crunching back along the cinder track."

"Must have been a tramp," said Meg, promptly. "Looking to see if the cottage was empty so that he could spend the night there. Or a stranded hiker, for that matter. Anybody."

"That's what I told her," said Isabel eagerly. "But she said it couldn't have been. She said they weren't the footsteps of a tramp, they—it sounds silly, but this is what she says. She says she recognised them."

"Well, whose were they, then?" asked Meg practically. "Didn't she tell you?"

"Yes. She told me." Isabel spoke gravely. "I don't know what to think, Meg. She says they were Uncle Paul's."

"Uncle *Paul's*? But Uncle Paul is—" Meg stopped, the words only half spoken. Because, of course, Uncle Paul wasn't dead—not so far as they knew. She had quite forgotten, after all these years, that Uncle Paul wasn't dead. Queer to think that, somewhere in the world, he was still existing . . .

"But it couldn't be Uncle Paul," she amended. "Uncle Paul is still in—"

But that might not be true either, as Isabel, with a sort of headlong diffidence, hastened to remind her.

"We don't *know* that he still is," she pointed out. "I mean, as Mildred says, after fifteen years . . . That's just the length of time . . ."

Yes, it was just the length of time. Meg hadn't thought of that. A life-sentence doesn't actually last for a life-time.

"But, Isabel, it's fantastic!" she protested. "After all this time! And why *should* he? I mean, he'd surely want to start a new life—keep right away from it all. He'd have even more cause than Mildred to want to put it all behind him."

"Mildred doesn't think so," insisted Isabel, heavily. "I told her all that. Just what you've said. But she says no, he will come back. He will come back to take his revenge, she says."

For a moment Meg felt horribly credulous; helpless in the grip of possibility. For she seemed to be looking once again into Uncle Paul's queer dark eyes, so melancholy, and yet so alert. How still he had stood as he surveyed the small girl in the doorway. She remembered the cool strength of the white hand that had taken her small red one with such courtly skill. She remembered the smooth black hair brushed shinily back from his pale forehead; the caressing, slightly foreign voice with which he had greeted her, Mildred's little sister . . .

"But it's absurd!" she burst out, common-sense reasserting itself. "It's just silly! As if anyone could recognise footsteps that they haven't heard for fifteen years—and in the middle of the night, too, when they're half drugged with sleeping tablets, as you say she was! It's ridiculous! And Mildred must know it is, too, in her heart, or she'd go to the police. Honestly, Isabel, if she really believed a single word of it, can you imagine that she'd go on staying all by herself in a lonely cottage on a cliff? Would anybody, let alone Mildred! I'll tell you what is it——" Meg was warming to her theme—"She's just dramatising herself the way she does—working herself up into a phoney panic so that everyone'll be sorry for her—and at the same time she'll have a good excuse for moving into a comfortable hotel, with bathrooms and hot meals. After all, when you've just told everybody that you're going to live the simple life and commune with Nature, you have to find *some* face-saving reason for packing it in after forty-eight hours. Just find her a nice, luxurious room in the best hotel in town, and you won't hear any more about foot-steps. You see!" Meg felt quite buoyant with that delicious sense of having solved someone else's problem without so much as lifting a finger. Even Isabel brightened a little.

"Do you think so, Meg? Do you really think so? It would be such a relief! And if you could only convince *her* that it's all nonsense—"

"I shan't try," retorted Meg briskly. "There'd be no point, because she knows very well that it's all nonsense, I'm certain she does. Trying to call her bluff like that would only make her play it up harder than ever. No; just find her a room in a good hotel. Go now, if you like. I'll look after the children."

Isabel shook her head hopelessly, and her shoulders drooped. For a moment Meg thought she would have to go through her arguments all over again; then she realised that Isabel's facile anxiety was by now focused in another direction.

"They *look* at you so," she was saying. "As if they think you're mad, coming and asking for a room in the middle of the season. And the big hotels—the kind Mildred would be happy in—you have to go across those miles of carpet to get to the enquiry desk, and I didn't bring any stockings, because it seemed silly for a camping holiday—I mean this is camping, really, isn't it, it's no different, except that you can stand up straight instead of having to crawl about—"

Meg burst out laughing.

"Isabel! Stop it! You'll get stuck like it one of these days! Listen: *I'll* find her a hotel. Right now. I'm sure it's not impossible—people must sometimes cancel at the last minute—get ill—something. Don't you worry. We'll soon have her fixed up with the kind of smart, sophisticated holiday she'll really enjoy. But remember, she'll want to feel that she's been *made* to do it—that we've forced her to leave the cottage against her will. Then she can tell herself ever afterwards that if only it hadn't been for us she'd have stayed there for weeks, finding it utterly divine, earwigs and all."

"I do believe you're right," said Isabel, her face brightening each moment as more and more of the responsibility seemed to be sliding from her shoulders on to Meg's. "Oh, it's such a comfort to have you here, Meg. You're the only one of us who really understands Mildred."

Meg smiled, a little complacently. She could not guess then how soon, and in what circumstances, she would be recalling those words of Isabel's.

CHAPTER IV

But I've *paid* for the cottage," Mildred was insisting, with a fine show of obstinacy. "I've paid for it for three weeks. I've no intention of being driven out of it by *anything*."

But her eyes, Meg noted, were already glancing with surreptitious appreciation at the shining seaside shops; her high heels, though still bearing traces of their recent walk over the cliffs, were now clicking confidently along the pavement, like two little exiles speaking their native tongue at last.

"Of course, I know you meant well, Meg," continued Mildred, pausing for a barely perceptible moment in front of a select and pink-shaded hairdresser's, "but you shouldn't—you really shouldn't—have actually booked the room for me. They'll make me pay for it, you know. People seem to think I'm *made* of money."

Since Mildred appeared to spend a large part of her life trying to induce people to think this very thing, Meg found the complaint unanswerable; she merely assured Mildred all over again that the room was not actually booked; it was merely awaiting Mildred's decision. "And we'd better hurry," continued Meg, quickening her pace past the huge store, which, like a great crystal ambush, lay in wait for just such as Mildred—"They said they couldn't keep it after midday, and I was to bring you to look at it as quickly as I could."

The Sea View Private Hotel was not, after all, the sort of place so dreaded by the stocking-less Isabel. Indeed, Meg was afraid at first that Mildred's first sight of it might undo all the effect of the shops and the bright streets. The entrance was an ordinary, and rather shabby, front door, leading into an ordinary narrow hall—seeming narrower than ever at this hour in the morning, when it was filled with the spades, children, towels and sandshoes of those families who were still in the throes of that prolonged occupation known as Getting Down to the Beach.

But there was an appetising smell of roasting meat coming from somewhere in the basement—*really* roasting meat, spitting and sizzling; not the silent, flabby pink lump you get out of a real old-fashioned cottage oven after you have spent the entire morning coaxing it with damp and insufficient supplies of real home-sawn logs. And in the lounge there were real armchairs, well-sprung and well-upholstered. No sign here of carved oak settles, whose unyielding hardness has triumphantly outlived so many generations of mere human spines . . . No antique rocking-chairs with one rocker more antique than the other if you put your weight on it . . . Cautiously, Meg observed her sister taking in all these satisfactory facts. Mildred's practised eye was already assessing those armchairs; fastening acquisitively on the most comfortable one . . . the one nearest the electric fire . . . and with the light comfortably placed behind it . . . and Meg knew that the battle was over.

"Though of course," insisted Mildred, after inspecting the comfortable little bedroom, "I still shan't give up the cottage. I shall go up there for the whole day sometimes. Quite often. I need the peace, you know, after all I've been through. The solitude. I feel cramped—imprisoned—by all this artificiality."

She gestured vaguely towards the mirror, and the basin with its hot and cold water. Meg hid a little smile. The very lips that were uttering these words were artificially coloured with the newest shade of lipstick; the very eyes that condemned were mascara'ed and shadowed with painstaking artifice; the head that nodded its disapproval was crowned by hair recently dyed chestnut.

"Of course. See how things go," agreed Meg, with the hearty but vague acquiescence of one whose interests lie in avoiding argument. She had little doubt now of the outcome. The phrase "Spend the day there" would soon turn into "Go for a stroll in that direction": and after that the subject of the cottage would fade altogether from Mildred's conversation.

Back in the lounge, in a different dress and different shoes, Mildred already seemed to belong to the place. She moved with a proprietary air towards the armchair that she had already mentally assigned to herself—and then stopped, with a look of affront that nearly made Meg giggle aloud. For now the precious armchair was occupied—or, at least, the seat of it was occupied—by a pack of patience cards laid out for a game of Picture-Frame. In front of the chair crouched a boy of about twelve, frowning intently as he fingered a five of spades; and leaning over him, remote and unheeded as a guardian saint, his mother gabbled patiently.

"Come along, Dear. Hurry up and finish, Dear. It's a shame to waste a nice morning like this indoors. Look at the sunshine, Dear. We ought to be down on the beach long ago. Haven't you nearly finished, Dear? It's such a pity to waste the fine weather. Come along, Dear."

"Yes, Mother," said Dear, placidly, and without moving a muscle. The five of spades would have to go on the rubbish heap after all. A pity, when the three and the two and the ace were all there waiting to be used . . .

"Excuse me—if your son wouldn't *mind* using the table . . . ?

At Mildred's words the guardian saint grew flustered to her very hair:

"You see, Dear? I told you not to set it out just when we were starting for the beach. Now, come *along*, Dear. I'm so sorry—" she turned to Mildred. "I'm so terribly sorry, but he'll clear it up at once, won't you, Dear, it won't take him a minute—"

Or an hour, either. Or a day. It was all the same to Dear.

"Yes, Mother," he repeated contentedly, moving a nine of clubs up to the centre; and Mildred tightened her lips.

"If I might be allowed to sit *down* . . ."

"Of course—of course! He's just going to clear them up this minute—" The mother's voice now held a piping, panicky note, like a lost soul; and Meg judged it time to intervene.

"You can't possibly get it out now; both your eights of diamonds are buried," she announced authoritatively. "You'll have to shuffle it up and start again." Sweeping the cards from the seat of the chair, she piled them pell-mell on to a small polished table nearby.

"I wasn't trying to get it out, actually," observed the boy, crushingly. "I was just working out the probabilities——" However, he made no further protest, but with dignity removed himself from the combat area, and proceeded to settle himself and his cards in another quarter of the room.

Neither Mildred nor the mother seemed as grateful to Meg as might have been expected at this summary solution to their problem; they both eyed her with a cautious hostility which suggested that it was *their* game she had spoiled, just as much as the boy's. And perhaps she had? Perhaps, in a place like this, it was as important to have something to complain of, some vitalising focus of conflict, as it was to have a comfortable seat.

However, victory is victory; and the best armchair, even more indubitably, is the best armchair; and Mildred was soon comfortably settled with a pile of magazines and with a hot lunch to look forward to in the not too distant future.

Meg took her leave, and set off along the sea front in the direction of the caravans. This is the first time since I got here, she reflected, in some little surprise, that I've actually seen the sea. You can't see it from the caravans at all, although it's so close, because of all the other caravans; and further on you can't see it because of the bathing huts; and after that you can't see it because of the parked cars and the sweet kiosks. The sea is like an animal kept at the zoo: you have to go in by a special entrance . . . Open Bank Holidays and Sundays . . . Please do not feed the Sea . . .

She expressed something of these thoughts to Isabel, whom she met some minutes later hurrying down to the beach with a bag containing buns, towels, sun-glasses, raincoats, comics, extra woollies and a piece of lemon-coloured plastic sheeting. The more Isabel carried in her bag, the more harassed she tended to look; and far from being amused by Meg's whimsical notion, she looked, for a moment, quite stricken.

"Oh, Meg, I wish you hadn't said that!" she exclaimed. "It reminds me of—Oh, I don't know! All those rows and rows of caravans, whichever way you look. It's worse than a street, really, because at least in a street there's a one side and another side—if you see what I mean," she added, rather hopelessly.

"Can we bathe as soon as we get there, Mummy?"

Isabel darted an anxious glance, not at Johnnie nor at the sea, but back towards the caravans as though the answer to Johnnie's question was to be found among the dry, tired shingle over which they had walked; somewhere among the curled, crisp bits of old orange peel, the scraps of blue chocolate paper and the broken shells, washed only by the winter tides.

"Yes—that is—yes, I think so, Johnnie. But come along; we must hurry!"

She quickened her pace, laboriously. They had the whole day before them, and so, Meg concluded, this haste must just be one of Isabel's anxious habits—one of those many uncomfortable little traits which this second marriage of hers seemed so to have emphasised.

"When's Philip coming back?" Meg asked, following her train of thought perhaps a little unguardedly; but Isabel appeared not to hear her; she hurried on, her head bent down against the sunshine as most people bend their heads against the rain; and in a few minutes they were out on the sands.

"This is our Place," said Isabel, rather bleakly, dumping down her bag beside the breakwater; and then picked it up again as the sand squelched beneath it. "But it seems wetter this time. I don't know why."

"Well, let's go farther up," said Meg, looking round for an empty space among the encamped families, who had by now ranged themselves with an extraordinary degree of equi-distance all over the beach. "Look—up by that concrete sort of thing, where it's all powdery and dry."

But going to a different Place seemed more of an undertaking than anyone as inexperienced as Meg could have anticipated. The sand wouldn't be right; and the distance from the sea wouldn't be right; and only two encampments away would be the Horrid Boy—the one who trod on things, and gave endless, unasked advice about moats.

And Isabel was, if anything, even more conservative than her sons. The thought of a new Place seemed to throw her into a flutter of miscellaneous forebodings. The direction of the wind; the safety of the children; the impossibility of seeing the pier clock—after a few minutes of this, Meg herself began to feel appalled at the immensity of the change she had proposed; and humbly enough she helped Isabel to spread out the raincoats and the bit of plastic sheet on the damp sand of the Place.

By the time they had finished their bathe the sun had gone, and a cold, inhospitable wind was whipping among the deckchairs. The whole beach was astir with people bending down to pull woollies out of their bags, and turning their chairs this way and that to modify the chill. Isabel cowered closer into the Place; Johnnie dripped his wet bathing suit into the bag of buns; and Meg proposed an immediate return to the caravan.

But this, apparently, could not be. They had only just come, Isabel explained, and they hadn't had their buns yet. And it wasn't as if it was actually *raining*, she pointed out, conclusively but without triumph, rather as one might point out to some hopeful invalid that he hasn't got a temperature and can go back to work.

This, for the moment, seemed unanswerable; and Meg reached out resignedly towards the bag of sandy buns that Isabel was holding out. Then, noticing that there were only three, she withdrew her hand.

"No—do take it," Isabel encouraged her. "It's meant for you. I never bring one for myself, because Peter doesn't eat his. He likes to be given it, you see, with everyone else, and then, when he doesn't eat it, I have it."

The contemplation of this depressing little manoeuvre seemed to cheer Isabel quite astonishingly, and she began to ask after Mildred and her new quarters.

"Oh, she's fine." Meg was cheerfully confident. "I left her in the best armchair, eyeing the other inhabitants in quite her old style. It's exactly what I said—now she's back in the comforts of civilisation, she can't be bothered any more with footsteps and shadows from the past. Besides, she's got a promising feud lined up already. About the armchair. That ought to give her all the drama she wants for days to come. And if that should fizzle out, there's always the guest who keeps on opening windows—or is it shutting them? I can never remember. Anyway, I told her we'd come over and see her soon; but it'll have to be you, actually, Isabel, because I have to be back at work first thing on Monday—"

Isabel had stopped munching. Peter's bun, with the currants and shiny top licked off it, waited motionless, three inches from her lips. Her face, pinched and cold from her recent bathe, was turned towards Meg with an expression of dismay quite inconsistent with the comfortable news Meg had supposed she was conveying.

"What on earth's the matter?" asked Meg; and then, rather irritably, for she, too, was cold: "I do wish you'd put that bun down; it isn't really helping you to be horrified. It just looks silly."

"I'm sorry." Isabel lowered her hand with a nervous little laugh. "It's stupid of me, Meg, but I hadn't realised you were going away at once. I mean, I know you said you'd come for the weekend, but I didn't know you meant it so literally. I thought you'd stay with me and see it through."

"But I *have* seen it through!" declared Meg, impatiently. "I told you—Mildred's perfectly all right now. When she gets sick of that little hotel—which I daresay she will soon—then she'll go back to Hubert. Yes, yes, I know she's never going to speak to him again, not even if he comes to her on his bended knees—but he won't; he'll come in a Rolls, just when her money's running out. There's no point in my staying any longer. I suppose I *could* take next week as part of my holiday, but—"

"Oh, *could* you, Meg? Could you really? Oh, if only you'd do that—!"

Meg did not know quite why she gave in—why she always gave in, to either of her sisters' pleadings. Not, surely, because she was a weaker character than they. On the contrary, was it not her very strength that forced her, the youngest, into this rôle of protector to them both?

Isabel's gratitude was disarming. Meg could not help laughing.

"Anybody would think that I'd saved your life!" she chided gaily; and wondered, a little, that Isabel did not smile in answer.

CHAPTER V

It was a little tiresome, thought Meg, that however wet you were, however cold and tired, you still had to scream and rub your ankle as you went up the caravan steps. And, moreover, she had only herself to blame. For was it not she, herself, who had first suggested to Peter that there were sharks to be fished for under those steps? Would a more experienced aunt, she wondered, have realised at once that this momentary inspiration for keeping her nephew amused would have this prolonged and wearisome aftermath? That Sharkey, in the form of a battered twist of plastic clothes line, would dwell for evermore beneath those steps, and demand his tribute of hollow cries and simulated terror? And you couldn't just hurry up the steps, screaming briskly, and be done with it. Oh no; you had to wait while Peter extricated himself from his pushchair and clambered under the steps to arrange Sharkey in his most menacing pose; and then you had to wait another chilling minute while Sharkey wriggled limply on the grass, uttering shrill, hissing cries like a repressed steam-engine, and finally, after many fruitless gyrations in the hands of his master, flipped feebly against your ankle. Then, and only then, were you allowed (indeed compelled) to utter your screams of terror and escape up the steps. If, in the hope of curtailing this ritual by some precious seconds, you screamed too early, while

Sharkey was still writhing on the ground, you were merely sent back to the bottom of the steps to begin all over again.

And it was worse still, mused Meg, when you had to queue up for the performance. Watching Isabel dutifully rubbing her ankle, and enunciating "Ow, ow, ow" Meg wondered bemusedly if it were perhaps different if you were the mother. Perhaps some preliminary softening of the rational faculties was as necessary to the whole business as the swelling of the breasts in preparation for suckling?

"Ow, ow," she was beginning resignedly, in her turn, when an exclamation, sharp and sudden, brought the performance to an end, even Sharkey falling meekly to the ground in mid-attack.

"Someone's been here!"

Isabel, turned to face them in the doorway above, was looking shaken, and she clutched her bulging bag to her body as if for mutual protection. "Someone's been sitting on my bunk!"

Meg burst out laughing.

"I'm sorry!" she apologised, breathlessly, hurrying up the steps to her sister. "But you sounded just like Mother Bear! What do you mean, someone's been here? How can you tell?"

The question was justifiable. Indeed, any outside observer might have found it hard to conceive that any form of intrusion, from a smash-and-grab raid downwards, could have increased the chaos habitual to Isabel's caravan. But, like most untidy people, Isabel had a very clear idea of the invisible order which (for the perpetrator) underlies even the wildest confusion.

"They've been sitting on my bunk," she insisted. "I know, because when I didn't make the beds this morning I didn't pick the pillows up either, and now two of them are back on the bed. And *I* didn't pull the rug over it like that . . . or take Johnnie's matchbox-tops off it . . . or . . ."— Isabel's voice became shrill again at this new discovery—"*I* didn't cook any scrambled eggs! Look!" With a clatter of disregarded crockery she yanked a saucepan from the pile of utensils awaiting washing up. "Look! It's had scrambled eggs in! All stuck to the bottom. See?"

Meg looked. Scrambled eggs it certainly was—or rather had been.

"And they haven't even put it to soak!" continued Isabel distractedly. "How am I ever going to get it clean now? And without hot water—"

With practised skill, Meg steered her sister back to the point.

"I should think Philip must be back," she suggested. "He must have cooked himself some lunch and then gone to look for you on the beach. What's so odd about it?"

But Isabel only stared at her, in irritating bewilderment.

"Philip?" she repeated, as if she had never heard the name before. "Philip? Oh no. It couldn't be Philip."

Her bland and unexplained rejection of Meg's common-sense suggestion was infuriating.

"*Why* couldn't it be Philip?" Meg demanded. "You said yourself he might be coming back today. What's the matter with you?"

But Isabel, fluttering and suspicious as a bird whose

nest has been tampered with, had spied yet another alien feature.

"The clothes!" she exclaimed. "The jerseys and pants I hung out before we went. They've been brought in! All folded in a pile, here." She pressed one of the offending garments to her cheek. "They're dry, too," she observed, as if this added, somehow, to the enormity of the interference.

"It *must* be Philip——" began Meg again; but was silenced—indeed stunned—by the violence with which Isabel turned on her.

"It can't be!" she almost shrieked. "I *told* you it can't be! He—he——" she stopped, flushed, and with a curious swallowing movement seemed to recover her self-control. "I'm sorry, Meg—I didn't mean to shout at you. It's just that—well—there isn't a train . . . I mean he couldn't be here so early . . . that is . . ." she gave a quick look round, as if to assure herself that the children were out of hearing; but having done so, all she said was: "I simply must tidy up a bit. If Philip *were* to come, and found it like this . . . and all Johnnie's comics . . . He was brought up very strictly, you know—Philip, I mean. He was never allowed to buy comics at all, and so he *does* rather——"

"Coo-ee, dear! You there?"

The cheerful slightly intrusive voice brought Isabel's rather rambling discourse to an end; and with a nervous, wholly ineffectual pat at her damp and untidy hair, she turned to greet the newcomer—turned to face her perhaps would be the better expression, for rarely had Meg seen anyone look so much like an animal at bay.

"*There* you are, dear!" cried Mrs Hutchins, surging up the steps with every blonde curl a-quiver. "I thought you must be back, and then when I saw the kiddies—Oh, by the way, love, I hope you don't think it was a bit of cheek, but I took your washing in for you. Looked as if it might rain, and I can't bear to see a nice dry bit of washing all getting wet again. No matter whose it is, I can't bear to see it. Funny, isn't it?"

Isabel's mouth smiled the casual gratitude due for such a service; while her eyes, as if harnessed to a different soul, registered only the mounting fear that perhaps, henceforth, *she* would be expected to take in Mrs Hutchins' washing when it looked like rain? Was, perhaps, already being criticised for not having done so in the past? And then, as Meg watched, all else was wiped from her sister's face by the realisation that Mrs Hutchins must have been inside the caravan and seen the state it was in.

"We set out terribly early this morning, before I'd done any of the work—" Isabel plunged headlong into complex and unskilful falsehood—"It's so lovely first thing, don't you think, we didn't want to miss it . . . And so we thought we'd have an early bathe and tidy up afterwards . . ."

Deeper and deeper into her morass of contradictory fabrications plodded Isabel, floundering this way and that as she stumbled up against such recalcitrant facts as that Mrs Hutchins must have seen her setting off for the beach at a quarter to twelve. Really, thought Meg, sheer practice alone should by now have made Isabel better at telling these ridiculous lies.

But, as it turned out, Isabel suffered no worse fate than is common to most liars; namely, the loss of her audience through the sheer dullness of her fabrications. Long before the narrative was finished, Mrs Hutchins had turned the whole of her not inconsiderable attention on to Meg.

"You just arrived, dear? You're the sister, aren't you, the one that works in town. Insurance, or something? My hubby, he used to be in Insurance. When he come out the Army. But he never took to it, not really. Promotion was too slow, he always said, but I don't reckon you want to worry about that, not while you're young, like you are. There's plenty else to think about while you're young, that's what I always say."

She giggled, vaguely, bored herself by the pointlessness of the innuendo, and reverted, with feigned casualness, to the topic which had really brought her here:

"By the way, there was a gentleman round this morning, looking for you two ladies. Find you all right?"

"Why—no—who was he?" began Meg; and simultaneously Isabel: "Not my husband? It wasn't my husband, was it, Mrs Hutchins?"

"Well, I wouldn't like to say. It isn't as if we've seen such a lot of your hubby, is it, dear, with him popping off to town such a lot. I haven't really seen him, you know, only the once. A dark gentleman, isn't he, middling height and a moustache? Or hasn't he a moustache? See what I mean? I'm no good at faces, no good at all." Mrs Hutchins spoke with the modest pride which everyone, for some reason, displays when claiming this particular incapacity. Then, fearing that the subject

48

of the mysterious gentleman might fizzle out for lack of data on her side, she was obliged to modify the splendid depths of her inability to remember faces:

"I'd have said this chappie was a bit younger than your hubby, dear," she ventured, with an unsuccessful attempt at uncertainty. "Though he was dark all right. Very dark. And about the right size, too, I should say." She stared at Isabel speculatively, as if one could assess the exact size of a husband by a sufficiently careful study of his wife.

"And a moustache? Did you say he had a moustache?"

Meg could hear the tenseness in Isabel's voice: Mrs Hutchins apparently could not, for she continued, as casually as ever: "Oh no, dear, I didn't say that. I only said I thought your hubby had a moustache."

The subject of the moustache seemed as if it would go on, at cross-purposes, for ever, neither Isabel nor Mrs Hutchins seeming capable of giving it a decisive function in the argument; so Meg intervened briskly:

"Did he speak to you? Leave any message? And" (with sudden recollection) "had he been scrambling eggs?"

Mrs Hutchins stared, helplessly, and a little aggrieved. By what features, she seemed to be wondering, could you be expected to recognise that a man had (or had not) been scrambling eggs? Meg realised that she had in some obscure way discomposed her informant and hastened on: "I mean, we were wondering, my sister and I—as soon as we came in we noticed that someone had been in the caravan, and we found that they'd been cooking scrambled egg. In a saucepan."

Mrs Hutchins shook her head, still helplessly. The scrambled egg had evidently put her right off her stroke, and in an uneasy sort of way she was blaming Meg for it.

"I don't know, I'm sure," she began, deflated; and then, suddenly, her curls once more began to quiver, and she became taut, plump and vigorous again:

"There he is!" she cried, pointing, forgetful of the laboriously acquired manners of her youth, along the lane between the caravans. A dark, trim figure, looking very out of place in its neat town suit and shiny shoes, was moving towards them with a sprightly grace that Meg at least knew well.

"Freddy!" she cried; and went on to greet him with the words uppermost in her mind rather than those most suitable to the occasion: "Have you been cooking scrambled eggs? And how on earth did you get here?"

Freddy's answer to this last question was forestalled by the necessity of introducing him to Isabel and Mrs Hutchins; his answer to the first, however, was full and explicit. Yes, he admitted, with a disarming smile at Isabel, it *was* he who had scrambled the eggs; and he did hope that she didn't mind. Her caravan, he explained, had reminded him so much of his sister's studio, where everyone dropped in to scramble eggs whenever they felt like it, at any hour of the day or night. He apologised most charmingly for taking such a liberty—at least, one could only presume that he was doing it charmingly, for his actual words were immediately drowned by Isabel's rival apology for not having invited him to lunch herself . . . for not having been there when he arrived . . . for everything being in such a mess . . . for the weather being so dull . . .

When Isabel's self-reproaches reached this degree of irrelevance, Meg always interrupted, on principle. She was on the point of doing so on this occasion when Isabel, suddenly and surprisingly, stopped of her own accord. Even more surprisingly, she began to laugh.

"How idiotic!" she exclaimed. "Meg, why don't you stop me?" and then, turning back to Freddy: "But what would you have done, Mr—er—Oh, all right, Freddy. What would you have done, Freddy, if it had turned out to be the wrong caravan? I mean, you couldn't have been sure, just from a cardigan that looked like Meg's."

"No caravan need turn out to be the wrong caravan if it is entered in the right spirit," pronounced Freddy gravely; and Isabel, astonishingly, rose to his banter.

"And what is the right spirit for entering my caravan?" she asked, with a gravity equal to his own; and Meg felt both pleased and surprised that the two of them seemed to be getting on so well.

She continued to be surprised, though progressively less and less pleased, as the afternoon went by, and Freddy stayed firmly at Isabel's side, laughing and talking with her, and paying the barest minimum of attention to Meg. He threw himself with extraordinary zest into Isabel's preparations for a family afternoon on the beach; and, once there, he agreed with apparent alacrity that Meg should go and bathe again with the children while he and Isabel settled down in the Place. The tide was out—out, indeed, almost to vanishing-point; and when Meg returned, mottled with cold from partial and intermittent immersion in eight inches of water, followed by a quarter-mile walk through the wind in her wet bathing suit, she found the two of them warm and laughing, and the Place hardly seeming like a Place at all. Admittedly, Johnnie's wet towel and Peter's stubbed toe soon did something to restore the familiar atmosphere; but even in this field Freddy seemed determined to excel. He bought them each a choc-ice, carried Peter home on his shoulders, and, on reaching the caravan, gave a most satisfactory display of terror at the onslaughts of Sharkey. Indeed, he not only screamed and rubbed his ankle in the approved manner, but actually fell flat on the ground with shrieks of most realistic agony. Meg looked on without enthusiasm at this addition to the repertoire.

"I suppose you realise," she remarked, a trifle acidly, "that now we'll *all* have to do that, every time, as well as rubbing our ankles?"

Freddy sat up and grinned at her.

"Poor old Auntie!" he sympathised. "What you need is a nice cup of tea. Why don't you go and make us all one?"

So saying, he lay back on the grass once more, closing his eyes against the sun which had burst through the clouds in belated evening glory.

Isabel was pottering ineffectually inside the caravan, as usual. Or, rather, not quite as usual, for her inefficiency now had a dreamy, contented quality. She seemed perfectly happy striking match after match and holding them to the gas burner that wouldn't work; and when Meg snatched them from her she looked quite surprised.

"Try rubbing two sticks together," advised Meg, sourly. "Meanwhile, I suppose *I'd* better make the tea." She lit the good burner, which leapt into life with an irritable pop that matched her mood exactly; while Isabel padded amiably down the steps to join Freddy outside in the sunshine.

Alone with the noisy, fussy little stove, Meg reviewed her grievances. Why had Freddy turned up like this, uninvited and unannounced, and with no explanation whatever? Being Bohemian was all very well, but there was such a thing as good manners. Poor old Auntie, indeed! Even as she fumed, Meg was aware that Freddy's unconventional behaviour would have been wholly forgiven—indeed, it would not even have struck her as unconventional—if he had only given the impression that he had come to see her, Meg, instead of flirting with Isabel all the afternoon. And the annoying thing was that Isabel wasn't really Freddy's type at all. Freddy liked smart, sophisticated women—or so he claimed; and yet here was Isabel, with her untidy hair, her ill-fitting cotton frock, her drab, anxious ways—

Bother! Isabel *would* have a whistling kettle that, instead of whistling, spat a jet of boiling water a yard across the room without warning. Meg dabbed briefly at her scalded knuckles; and it was in no very amiable manner that she stumped down the steps and planted the tea-things on to the rickety box that served as an outdoor table.

"Hullo, sweetheart? Did you get out of the sea on the wrong side this afternoon?"

Freddy beamed at her provokingly; but Meg was in no mood for repartee.

"When's your train?" she asked baldly. "Have you time for a cup of tea?"

"Oh, yes. Lots of cups." Freddy was reassuring. "I'm staying here, you know."

"Staying?" Meg hadn't meant to display any interest, but she had herself found such difficulty in getting a room for Mildred that she could not help asking the question. "Where are you staying? And why?" she added, hastily, remembering that she was cross with him.

Freddy seemed to meditate his answer.

"As to why," he said at last, "you might as well ask the same question of all the miserable, cold, quarrelsome people who face a fortnight of such a place every year of their lives. Out of all those millions, why pick on *me*? But as to where, that's easier. I'm staying at a hotel. My window," he added, politely informative, "is marked with a cross."

CHAPTER VI

"I like your Freddy," observed Isabel, rather superfluously. "But who is he, exactly?"

The sun had set, and the vast peace of summer twilight was managing to filter through the shouts and the wireless sets as irresistibly as mist through the cracks in a door. Meg and Isabel were sitting on the steps of their caravan, blissfully free, at this hour, from the importunities of Sharkey.

"Who is he, Meg?" repeated Isabel. "Freddy what?"

"I don't think he's Freddy anything," said Meg, a trifle obscurely. "I mean, he's down in the telephone book as R. J. Coleman, and you can't get Freddy out of that. I met him at a party about a month ago, and everyone was calling him Freddy, so of course I did too. I suppose that's how people do get called things," she added, vaguely, turning back to her book.

"You mean you've only known him a month?" Isabel was sounding tiresome again. "You ought to be careful, Meg."

"Well, I like that!" Meg laughed caustically at this some-what belated display of elder-sisterly caution. "I like that! *You've* only known him for half a day, and——"

But Isabel pursued her point with unusual doggedness. "I mean, Meg, you don't seem to know *anything* about him," she persisted. "What does he do, for instance? Who are his people?"

"I think he's quarrelled with them," said Meg, with dreamy tolerance. "Either that or he hasn't got any. And as to what he does, he's a pianist. Sort of," she added, after a moment's reflection.

"What do you mean, he's a pianist, *sort of*?" asked Isabel, rather belligerently. "Do you mean he *wants* to be a pianist? Or gives part-time lessons at a girls' school? Or what?"

Meg was beginning to realise, for the first time, how little she did in fact know about Freddy's life.

"I think he accompanies—or something," she said. "He sometimes talks about having engagements. And not having them. Things like that. *I* don't know—what *do* people usually do who call themselves pianists?"

"Clerical work, mostly," said Isabel gloomily, from her few years' longer experience of life. She resumed her catechism. "How old is he?"

"How you do keep on!" complained Meg. "It had never occurred to me that there *were* so many things to be known about a man. I've never asked him. Twenty-eight? Thirty? It's hard to tell."

"Almost impossible, nowadays. I'm sometimes decades out myself."

The voice, soft and mocking in the twilight, made both girls jump. Meg dropped her book under the steps, while Isabel scrambled ungracefully to her feet.

"Why, Freddy!" she exclaimed. "I—we—thought you'd gone home hours ago."

"I've come back," explained Freddy, settling himself amiably on the grass at their feet. "It's hard on the younger generation, isn't it?"

"What is?" Surprise seemed to have robbed Isabel of all her new-found poise. "What are you talking about?"

"Why—what you were just discussing—the difficulty of judging a person's age. I only mean that nowadays, when people of forty are just as likely as not to look twenty— well, it's hard on the ones who actually *are* twenty. Don't you find it so?"

Tactfully, he refrained from making it clear which sister he was addressing, and Isabel brightened once more.

"Like perms," she rejoined, with more eagerness than clarity. "I mean," she proceeded, rather laboriously, to explain, "it's hard on the girls who've got *naturally* wavy hair—"

"Anyway, I don't agree," interrupted Meg. "I don't think people can make themselves look young nowadays any more than they ever could. I mean, with make-up and so on a woman of forty can make herself look more attractive, but I don't think she necessarily looks younger—"

"Attractive but forty. How true," mused Freddy. "But you take me up too crudely, Meg. I don't mean anything as simple as that. Of course, a woman—or a man for that matter—may put on a disguise to represent this age or that, just as they always could. No; I mean that life nowadays no longer follows a set pattern, each decade bringing its own characteristic and predictable pleasures and troubles, marking the features in its own distinctive way. The carefree student; the earnest young husband; the responsible, over-burdened parent; they came in proper rotation, and left their appropriate mark. But now the rotation is all upset. The responsible and burdened parent of twenty-three will probably have divorced his wife and become a carefree student by the time he is forty. Naturally his appearance is misleading—"

"But could a person do it deliberately?" Isabel's interruption was clumsy and inappropriate in its intensity. "Could they pretend—acquire—the sort of characteristics—like you were saying—on purpose so you'd think they were ten years younger—older than they were? Could they? As much as ten years?"

She spoke almost fiercely, and as if much depended on the answer. Freddy must have been aware of this, for he sheered off the subject at once.

"You've been reading too many whodunits, my girl," he diagnosed lightly; and reaching under the steps, he pulled out the book that Meg had dropped. He peered at the title in the waning light.

"'Murder for Two'," he read out triumphantly. "I told you so!" and then, sounding a little aggrieved: "But I've read it. I thought it would be something I could borrow."

"You couldn't borrow it anyway," observed Meg. "It's mine, and I'm only half way through."

"If you're half way through, you're as good as finished," Freddy assured her. "As soon as the butler starts being so unnecessarily certain that he didn't put any logs on the fire—"

"Oh, stop it!" cried Meg, laughing. "I haven't even got

to the bit about the butler. They're still grilling Roderick's wife about where she went after the party; and she's got such a cast-iron alibi that I think it must be her."

"Don't be too sure. They tend to double-cross you nowadays," said Freddy darkly. "They know you're going to suspect the one with the cast-iron alibi, and so they make him be innocent, just to show you; while the murderer turns out to be the one who was seen creeping out of the library window at midnight and whose finger-prints are all over everything. Besides," he added, refreshing his memory by a glance at the final chapters, "wives are only put into a book to mislead. To think that their husband's done it when he hasn't, so that they can confuse everybody by telling a lot of lies to protect him—"

"But why?" suddenly burst out Isabel. "*Why* is it assumed that a wife will automatically protect her husband—or a girl her fiancé—if she thinks he's a murderer? Doesn't anybody realise how—how plain terrified she'd be? I don't care how much she loves him; if a thing like that happened she'd just simply be terrified. She'd have no other feelings at all. Doesn't anyone understand?"

For just one second Freddy seemed taken aback by this outburst. Then he grinned, and spoke with only a trifle less than his usual cheerful arrogance.

"My dear girl, don't look at me like that! *I* don't write the things. But if I ever do, I promise you I will attend to what you say. The wives shall betray their husbands promptly. All of them. I'll have them queueing up at the police station. Will that do?"

Isabel's laugh was forced. Meg did not speak at all. After a glance from one to the other of them, Freddy shrugged and got to his feet.

"Well—I suppose I'd better be going."

A note of bewilderment, of genuine disappointment, in his usually self-confident voice roused Meg.

"I'll walk along with you a bit," she offered, jumping up. It was growing dark now, and she could not see clearly the expression on his face. However, he took her arm after a second's hesitation, and led her swiftly towards the road.

"I'm sorry—I seem to have rather put my foot in it with your sister," began Freddy when they were out of earshot. "Has her old man been bumping off a rich uncle recently, or something?"

"No, oh no!" Meg laughed, from sudden unreasoning happiness rather than at Freddy's flippancy. "Philip? Oh no! On the contrary."

Freddy too laughed, apparently completely at ease again.

"And what *is* the contrary of bumping off a rich uncle?" he enquired. "It might be a useful thing to know."

"Oh—well, I only meant that Philip would be the last possible man you could imagine running amok in *any* way. I've only met him a few times myself, but he's a very obvious sort of type. You know—retired Army. Much older than Isabel, and very precise; very—well—fussy, really—wanting everything to be just so. As different from Isabel as he could possibly be. I can't imagine, really, how they—I mean, when you see how Isabel runs things—"

She stopped, aware of disloyalty; aware, too, that under all his flaunted light-heartedness, Freddy's feelings about disloyalty might be strong. "Isabel's such a happy-go-lucky sort of person," she finished feebly.

"Minus both happiness and luck, eh?" supplemented Freddy, smiling straight ahead of him into the darkness. "Suppose we sit down here, and you tell me what it is that's upsetting you both?"

They had come out on to the parade now, and he led Meg into a glass-sided shelter facing out across a sea so smeared and spangled by lights that it seemed as much a man-made structure as the parade itself.

"Now tell me what it's all about," commanded Freddy; and without forethought or caution, Meg in the darkness proceeded to tell him.

"It's something that happened when we were quite small," she began. "At least, I was quite small. Isabel must have been twelve or thirteen, I suppose—she was at boarding-school already, only she was home for the holidays when it all happened. Mildred had got engaged to a young man called Paul Hartman. At least," amended Meg, anticipating her climax, "that's what he called himself. I remember him coming to the house for the first time. He was quite different from any of our usual visitors, and I remember staring and staring. He was very elegant, very dark—rather slight, I realise now, though of course at the time he seemed to me quite tall. I'd never seen anything like his great liquid brown eyes and his dark arched eyebrows, extraordinarily clear cut against his white forehead. And his voice—"

"It sounds to me," interrupted Freddy, "as if, in your little innocent heart, you cherished a pretty sizeable crush on the gentleman."

"Well—yes—I suppose I did," laughed Meg. "And, you know, he *was* very charming, there's no getting away from it, in spite of what happened afterwards. What we found out afterwards, that is to say—it had all *happened* actually, before we ever saw him. Well, anyway, he made a dead set at Mildred, and she fell for him at once, and after a very few weeks they got married. "At least," Meg amended once more, "they had a wedding, and everyone—Mildred too, of course—*thought* they'd got married. But it turned out later—oh, only two or three weeks later, as far as I remember—the whole thing can only have taken the length of the summer holidays, because I remember how hot it was all the time, and how cool Uncle Paul—that's what Isabel and I called him—how cool he always managed to look while everyone else was baking. I suppose it was because he was naturally so pale—"

"Oh, get on, my sweet. Cut out the interesting pallor. *What* happened two or three weeks later?"

"It turned out that he was already married," said Meg. "And not only that, but the police were after him for the murder—the attempted murder—of his first wife. Apparently he'd married her for her money, got it made over to himself, and then taken her abroad and pushed her over a cliff. He must have thought he'd finished her off, but he hadn't; and when she got better—or maybe when she began to realise it couldn't have been an accident—I don't know—she set the police on his tracks. Just about the time when, under a different name, he was 'marrying' his next heiress—Mildred."

"Mildred an heiress, eh?"

Freddy had lighted a cigarette now, and the tip glowed motionless in the dark.

"Oh yes—I forgot to tell you. Mildred had—has—quite a lot of money left her by her own mother. That's why he fastened on her, of course. He was planning the same thing all over again."

"I see. But his plans were foiled, in spite of the false name. By whom?"

"It—it was Mildred," said Meg uncomfortably. "She—she found out somehow who he really was, and went to the police. He was arrested at our house early one morning, before breakfast. I remember waking up and hearing a lot of shouting and tramping of boots—but you know how it is when you're a child, everyone tells you not to worry, and everything will be all right: we never did find out exactly how it all happened. And it's no good asking Mildred, because she tells it differently every time, according to whether she wants to appear as the innocent young girl betrayed by a scoundrel, or as the astute amateur detective to whom police and public owe undying gratitude. Anyway, he was brought to trial, given a long prison sentence, and that was the end of it—or should have been; but now that his time is up, Mildred's been getting into a state about it all over again. And she's managed to get Isabel worked up about it as well—Isabel is so suggestible, you know—"

Here Meg related the story of Mildred's stay at the cottage; her terror at the mysterious footsteps, and her far-fetched suggestion that they might be Paul's.

"It sounds to me like a lot of hysterical nonsense," finished Meg. "But Mildred thinks—or, just for the drama of the thing, pretends she thinks—that Paul has come back to find her, and to take his revenge."

"Revenge." Meg wished that she had turned her sentence differently, so that this word had not come at the end, ringing solitary through the darkness. And what made it worse was that Freddy did not immediately answer. Dimly she could see his profile, staring out towards the battered brilliance of the tamed and defeated sea.

"Both of them," he said at last; and for a moment, in the darkness, Meg did not know to what he was referring.

"Both of your sisters," he continued. "It would seem that on this subject they are agreed. In real life, apparently, as Isabel was saying, women *are* quite ready to betray the man they love. I didn't know."

Meg knew, then, that she had told the story in too casual, too flippant a manner. It had jarred upon him. But—too flippant for *Freddy*? It wasn't fair of him to be so frivolous, so cynical nearly all the time, and then suddenly turn serious in unpredictable flashes like this. She felt snubbed, rebuked, and her determination to justify herself could only take the form of an exaggerated defence of Mildred.

"That's not fair!" she cried. "Not in Mildred's case. She didn't love him any more, you see. You can only talk about loyalty where there is a love to be loyal to. She hated him once she knew what he had done—and that he'd only wanted her for her money in any case. She just wanted to be rid of him. No, what was worrying her most, I think, was the sort of publicity it was getting. The papers didn't make her seem either a betrayed innocent or a super-sleuth—they just made it all sound sordid. They must have been full of it for weeks. Even I can remember it, though I can't have read papers much at that age. I do remember very clearly seeing a paper on the kitchen table with Uncle Paul's photograph in it. The photograph of him as he was, I mean, before he met Mildred. He'd disguised himself a bit since then, shaving off his moustache and so on, but I could still see the likeness. I remember covering the moustache with my finger, and seeing how exactly like the rest of it was; and then I went off into the garden to look for Uncle Paul to see if he really did look like that."

"But, of course, Uncle Paul wasn't there by that time; he'd be safe behind bars," said Freddy, staring in front of him.

"Well—yes. Now I come to think of it, he must have been," said Meg. "But it's funny, I seem to have a distinct recollection of finding him under the rose arch, smoking a cigarette and looking over the smoke at me in that queer, sparkling way he had. But it must nave been some other occasion, obviously."

"Obviously." Freddy took several more puffs at his cigarette. "And all this, you think, explains our Isabel's little outburst this evening?"

"Oh, yes." Meg was quite positive. "She was feeling rather—you know—on edge about Mildred's affairs altogether, and then you bringing up the subject of wives whose husbands are murderers—well, naturally it upset her. She was sort of defending Mildred—pointing out the conflict she must have faced. Though I don't think, actually, that Mildred ever saw it as a conflict at all, not in the way that Isabel would. I think she just saw it as an unsavoury situation to be escaped from as completely as possible—or sometimes to be dramatised, in suitable company. She's never been a person to look all round things, and worry, and weigh them up, as Isabel does."

"And you? Which sort of person are you?"

"Me?" Meg was startled. "How do you mean?"

"I mean," Freddy spoke carefully, "I mean, Meg, that if you had found yourself in Mildred's place, married—or as good as married—to this fascinating scoundrel—would *you* have gone to the police? And given evidence against him?"

No one could have been more surprised than Meg to find that she did not need to reflect on her answer for even a moment.

"Of course I wouldn't!" she cried. "I'd have kept it dark: I'd have told lie after lie. And if another murder was necessary to help him escape, I'd have committed it with him! There!"

She paused, breathless, astonished at her own vehemence. Freddy's eyes were fixed on her with extraordinary brilliance.

"You wouldn't, of course," he commented. "When it came to the point, you'd behave like any ordinary, sensible young woman. But it's pleasant—yes, it's quite remarkably pleasant—to know that, in your inexperience, you *think* you would."

CHAPTER VII

The lounge of the Sea View Private Hotel was full when Meg and Isabel, fulfilling their promise, arrived after lunch on the following day. Every chair was occupied, and over all brooded a guilty tranquillity. Everybody knew that they couldn't go on sitting like that much longer, for this was a holiday, and they mustn't waste it sitting about in the hotel. Even as Meg hesitated in the doorway, trying to locate Mildred among the somnolent throng, a sort of unhappy stirring was beginning.

"I think—in a few minutes—it would be all right to think about bathing, Dear," ventured the blonde and ineffectual mother whom Meg had encountered yesterday. Her son, to whose deaf ears this remark was being addressed, was no longer in possession of the best armchair. Instead, he and his patience cards were spread out to their fullest extent on the stretch of floor that everyone had to cross to reach either the writing table or the door. A further area to his left was also rendered impassable by three or four sheets of foolscap paper, ruled into columns, and filled from end to end with cramped, untidy figures.

"Or perhaps," his mother continued her soliloquy above his unresponsive torso, "perhaps it would be better to wait another quarter of an hour. You had rather a heavy lunch." Impassively, the youth writhed round to write another figure in his overflowing columns, and then began to shuffle the cards again, their edges clicking fussily on the polished boards. A small grey-haired woman peered down at him over her spectacles.

"There doesn't seem much point in bringing him for a holiday, does there, Mrs Forrester?" she observed with the forthright tartness of the elderly—of those, that is to say, who have become spectators of life rather than players, and are no longer responsible for the success of the show. "If all he wants to do is to read and play cards, he could do it just as well at home, surely? And much more cheaply."

"Oh, I know, Miss Carver, I know." Mrs Forrester wagged her head forlornly. "But, you see" (in a lower tone) "his father isn't—well, isn't living with us any longer, and I don't want poor Cedric to feel that he's missing anything. Especially as he'll be going on a visit to his father straight after," she added, rather irrelevantly—irrelevantly, at least, as it would seem to anyone unfamiliar with the weary competition for their child's approval which besets so many separated parents.

Miss Carver continued to look disapproving. Pointedly she withdrew her neatly laced foot as the tide of patience cards crept nearer.

"Well, I don't know," she said. "I'm not speaking personally, you understand, Mrs Forrester; but it does seem to me that the children nowadays don't enjoy their holidays as we used to do. To us, a seaside holiday really *was* a holiday. It was the only time when we could discard our black stockings and our petticoats, and run bare-legged in just a holland overall. You can't imagine—you can't *imagine*—what it was like to feel the sun on our bare legs for the first time!"

For a moment, the memory of that long-ago ecstasy illuminated Miss Carver's lined face, tautened her tired body as if in readiness for that first enchanted scamper across the sands of sixty years ago. Then, quickly, she recaptured the thread of her discourse:

"But nowadays, when children spend the whole summer with next to nothing on in their back gardens, and even in the street—well, naturally, half the point of going to the seaside has vanished. And then again, for us, a holiday meant a chance to be with our parents for much of the day. Ordinarily, you know, we were kept very strictly in the nursery, in the care of our nurse. We rarely met our parents on equal terms, as—"

Miss Carver stopped in mid-sentence. No doubt she had been going to say: "As children do nowadays"; but the sight of the untroubled figure on the floor, now whistling faintly through its teeth, must have daunted her. How could any parent, let alone this particular one, ever hope to be counted as the equal of this self-possessed creature, with his almost superhuman indifference to anyone's concerns but his own?

While listening with half her mind to this interchange, Meg had meanwhile been scanning the room for her eldest sister. She now caught sight of her, at the far end of the room. Mildred was not sitting on the coveted armchair this time, but on a sofa in the corner; and Meg saw that she was wearing the expression of fixed animation that meant she was talking to a man. In fact, Meg noticed the expression before she noticed the man, so small and insignificant did he seem beside Mildred's colourful presence. Meg was not a little surprised, therefore, that as she and Isabel moved in that direction, the insignificant little figure should suddenly burst into song:

"If the line AB is paral-lel to the li-ine CD—then the opposite a-angles are e-equal—" he carolled and then, returning to his normal, slightly falsetto voice, he continued: "Like that—every single thing I said during his lesson, he made me sing it! *Everything!* You can imagine what a fool I felt! But it worked, you know. Within a year, my stammer was cured. Completely. Except for just now and then if I'm n-nervous . . ."

His voice wavered as he saw Meg and Isabel bearing down upon them. Mildred also saw them, without, Meg fancied, very much pleasure.

"Oh—hullo, dears," she greeted them, rather perfunctorily. "I'd forgotten you were coming. Do sit down—er—somewhere. Oh—this is Captain Cockerill—" But the little captain was on his feet already, his beaming gallantry only a little marred by the impression he gave of being tangled up in his own legs as he attempted simultaneously to offer Isabel his own seat on the sofa, and to secure for Meg a spindly little chair which was so far successfully evading him on the other side of a polished mahogany table.

Tranquillity was finally restored, only, alas, to reveal that none of them could think of anything to say. "Do sing to us again" was the only thing that came into Meg's mind, but she discarded it as unlikely to ease the situation.

As so often happens, the uncomfortable little pause coincided with a lull in conversation all over the room; and the lull forthwith gathered momentum until it became a stony silence, as the remaining talkers, one after another, realised that their remarks could now be overheard by the entire company.

Now indeed came the test of courage; and, surprisingly enough (so unpredictable are the different brands of valour) it was Mrs Forrester who first spoke.

"I believe it's going to rain," she said.

This heroic pronouncement had the desired effect, and relief ran like a current of warmth through the lounge. It soon became apparent, too, that the relief was not due solely to the breaking of an awkward silence: there was an unmistakable look of furtive hope about many of the faces that turned with conventional concern towards the window. Was a comfortable afternoon of idleness in store for them after all?

"Oh dear, I'm afraid it *does* look rather unsettled," exclaimed a pale little woman, trying to disguise the satisfaction with which she unfolded again the embroidery which she had been dutifully putting away. "I fear" (with ill-suppressed eagerness) "I fear we must resign ourselves to an afternoon indoors."

"I fear so" . . . "Very threatening" . . . "I noticed the glass had fallen" . . . The chorus of guilty hope was swelling; library books were reopened with stealthy relief; feet were replaced on footstools; knitting-needles resumed their comfortable clicking.

And then, suddenly, all was shattered. It might have been the voice of Nanny herself, ringing across the decades:

"I think it's going to clear up," Miss Carver announced briskly. "It's just the day for a good walk." Heedless of the ruined hopes she was leaving behind her, Miss Carver gathered up her belongings and tripped out of the room.

No one's moral courage could stand up to this. A few last, forlorn glances were cast out of the window, where a streak of blue on the horizon was relentlessly growing bigger; and then the whole room, the whole house, was astir with preparations.

Captain Cockerill was gallantly anxious that Mildred and her two sisters should accompany him for a walk along the promenade; and Meg could only hope that the poor little man was prepared for the way in which this simple proposal, in the hands of Mildred and Isabel, at once took on the character of a large-scale manoeuvre. First, Mildred had to change into an entirely new outfit, including a different shade of nail varnish which took a quarter of an hour to dry. After this, Isabel had to decide whether or not to take her raincoat. This exhausting topic, which was apt at the best of times to reduce Isabel to quivering uncertainty, seemed on this occasion to be straining her powers of decision almost to the point of paralysis. For the question now depended not merely on whether or not it was going to rain, but also on whether or not they would be coming back to the hotel before returning to the caravan. The contemplation of this double set of pros and cons, combined with the conflicting advice of her three companions, was rapidly reducing Isabel to a pitiable state, in which she could neither stop talking about the raincoat nor fetch it from its peg: Meg had finally to come to the rescue by stating firmly that she, Meg, had no intention whatever of coming back to the hotel, and that the coat must, therefore, be brought with them.

But by this time Mrs Forrester, with the inconspicuous skill of the solitary holiday-maker, had managed to attach herself to the walking party; and so now they all had to wait while Cedric finished his patience, added up a column of figures nine inches long, and divided the answer by eighteen.

And so, at last, they set out, Captain Cockerill still evincing an undiminished enthusiasm for the expedition which, in the circumstances, was little short of heroic. The wind had risen; it was coming in from the open sea, cutting with damp ferocity across the parade where most people by now were cowering in shelters eating chocolate and waiting for it to be tea-time. But Captain Cockerill, daunted neither by the weather nor by his rather overpowering female escort, strode jauntily along, his head held high in defiance of his short stature, and with every appearance of enjoyment.

"Wonderful sight it must be in winter!" he exclaimed, gazing out enthusiastically over the grey tangle of water. "The sea comes right up over the parade, you know, during the winter storms."

"No, it doesn't," contributed Cedric—the first words he had uttered that afternoon. "It used to, but they built the parade higher five years ago. It's in the Guide Book."

"Oh. Ah." For one second Captain Cockerill seemed a little at a loss. Then, with renewed sprightliness, he turned to consult his rather depressed entourage about where they would like to go? A good tramp over the cliffs, perhaps? Or round the point to Whitesands Bay, if the tide wasn't too high?

"What about the Pier?" suggested Mildred, her whole soul expanding as she contemplated its nearness, its roofed-in parts, and the café at the end of it.

"Oh yes, the Pier!" Mrs Forrester clapped her hands with a display of girlish rapture that was only partly feigned, for she, too, was sustained by the same vision as Mildred. "Cedric will love the slot machines," she added, anxious to dispel any suspicion that she shared Mildred's middle-aged preference for comfort. "I'll give you a nice lot of pennies, Dear, and you can play with all the machines one after another."

Cedric glanced at his mother pityingly.

"They aren't any good," he explained patiently. "Unless you've got time to really study them, and work out how to get your money back every time. But," he added, with the air of one offering consolation to a disappointed child, "you can give me the money you would have given me for the slot machines and I'll put it in my savings."

But neither Cedric, nor the wind, nor his unenterprising companions seemed able to depress Captain Cockerill.

"The Pier it is!" he acquiesced brightly. "Here we are. See? The fourth longest pier on the South Coast. Built in 1875—"

"No, it wasn't," said Cedric. "It was in 1910. That notice is wrong. In 1875 they only——"

Meg did not hear the remainder of this dissertation. Indeed, the whole of the following hour remained in her memory almost as a blank, so numbed did she allow herself to become with cold and boredom. She remembered, vaguely, that the afternoon was coloured by Mildred's search for a cup of tea (the pier café had, as usual, proved to be closed); by Isabel's intermittent and profitless speculations as to whether they were leaving the children for too long; and by Mrs Forrester's wavering attempts to explain to Cedric why it was that they had had to come for the walk at all. Meg did not really rouse herself until, on their way home, they came across the Fortune-teller's booth.

It was Mildred who first noticed it.

"Oh, I must be done!" she cried, her mood, for the first time, matching her outfit—from the outset it had struck Meg as a pity to put on so new and colourful a suit just to look sulky in. "I *must* go in," continued Mildred. "How much do you think it costs? I don't seem to have brought my bag . . ."

Having thus extracted half a crown from the still valiantly smiling captain, Mildred disappeared inside the flapping canvas.

Disappeared for a long, long time. Long enough, at any rate, for the rest of the party (more in search of shelter from the wind than of entertainment) to explore the other booths in the vicinity. They achieved one sixpennyworth of warmth in the company of a South American coypu, billed as the Largest Rat in the World; and another, rather longer, in contemplation of the Sheep with Six Legs. Or sixteen—or sixty—the claim would have made no difference, since the creature remained obstinately lying down throughout their visit, staring at them with liquid, expressionless eyes. The Indian Snake Juggler proved little more exciting. A rather dusty looking cobra lay coiled on the floor in a dreamless sleep, while the juggler—a lady of indeterminate nationality touched up with walnut juice—reclined in a chair at its side, draped in emerald green and with shiny black ringlets drooping round her lack-lustre countenance. It seemed that neither she nor the cobra were required by the terms of their contract to show any signs of life; and so it was not long before the party trooped out into the cold again.

The irrepressible Captain Cockerill, however, seemed to have been quite excited by the dismal little spectacle, and the moment they got outside he began telling them about his time in India. "You wouldn't believe the things some of those chaps could do with cobras," he recalled. "They could make the blighters sway and wave their heads about in time to music. I've seen it myself. And sometimes one of these johnnies would get hold of a cobra by one end and hold it out stiff as a poker. A creature six or seven feet long, you understand. Marvellous! Some kind of hypnosis, I suppose."

"No, it isn't," said Cedric. "It's just a matter of pressing a certain part of the vertebra near the base of the head. It's quite easy. I could do it myself."

"You shouldn't talk like that, Dear," said his mother, vaguely, as if not quite sure what it was that she was reproving—the contradicting of his elders—the boasting about untried skills—or the mere idea of handling snakes at all. Not that it mattered which she meant, for Cedric, of course, was paying no attention to her at all.

"Cobras make very good pets," he was explaining, in his informative way. "They're very intelligent, and very tame, too, if you train them properly. You can get one for forty-five shillings."

The serene confidence with which he produced this esoteric and unverifiable piece of information was somehow too much for Meg.

"No, you can't," she snapped—at random, and for no other reason than to show him that even adults will turn at bay sometimes. "No, you can't. They cost about a hundred pounds."

The wildness of the guess made even her own voice falter. Cedric gazed at her pityingly.

"Where did you hear that?" he enquired; but happily, before Meg found herself provoked into asserting that she had been brought up on a snake farm in Central America, they were interrupted. Mildred, who had rejoined them some minutes ago, and had been waiting impatiently for a chance to claim the full attention of the company, could restrain herself no longer.

"My dears, she's marvellous!" she exclaimed, taking an arm each of Meg and Captain Cockerill. "She's simply wonderful! She seemed to know all about me straight away. Would you believe it, she told me right off that I was married to a man rich in this world's goods, but poor in understanding and sympathy!"—a single glance, Meg reflected, at Mildred's smart clothes and her discontented face, would be evidence enough of this—"And she said I was highly strung, and suffered from insomnia—" The trite catalogue continued to its foolish and foreseeable conclusion: "And so she says that for five guineas she can give me a really full reading. With a crystal. She says I'm the sort of person who'd be really worth while, because I have the right vibrations. But I'd have to go to her house, she says, because there's a fuss with the police if she uses a crystal here, and so—"

"Oh, Mildred, don't be so silly! Don't waste your money like that!" protested Meg; and she embarked with some warmth on the usual arguments of the rationalist. And with the usual results, too; for Mildred simply stared through her and past her, and kept repeating, with a sort of dreamy superiority: "You don't understand, dear."

And now Captain Cockerill must need chip in on the side of lunacy, with a series of unconfirmed and rather long-winded anecdotes about prophesies and forewarnings that he had encountered during his sojourn in India. At the end of which Isabel suddenly roused herself, as if from deep sleep, to say: "*India?* Did you say India, Captain Cockerill?"

Since Captain Cockerill had said "India" at least twelve times during the past half hour, one would have expected him to show at least a little irritation. Instead of which, he seemed delighted, and continued to beam happily throughout Isabel's inane query as to whether he mightn't have met her husband Philip? He'd been in India, too, some time or other, she explained.

"When were you there?" she concluded, in a belated attempt to bring the thing within the range of possibility.

"Let me see." Captain Cockerill treated the matter with courteous gravity. "I went out first in 1937—" Automatically he glanced with some trepidation at Cedric as he made this rash assertion, but meeting for once with no contradiction, he proceeded to enquire civilly about Philip's career.

But when it came to actual facts, Isabel was vague to a degree which made the subject even duller to the rest of the company than it would have been in any case. Fearing that Captain Cockerill might offer to escort them all the way to the caravan, bandying with Isabel these unpronounceable places and uncertain dates the whole way, Meg decided that they had better return to the hotel after all, and set off to the caravan by themselves later.

As they entered the hotel, they found a little crowd blocking up the entrance to the lounge. Voices were raised, in varying tones of reproach, envy and self-righteousness:

"What! *All* the afternoon? Shame on you!"

"And the electric fire on, too!"

"But it's been *lovely* out! So fresh!"

Curious to see who could be the intrepid spirit who had dared to defy tradition and public opinion to the extent of staying indoors when it wasn't actually raining, Meg squeezed her way through the throng and into the lounge. There, comfortably ensconced in the best armchair, with his feet up on the best footstool, and with the electric fire full on, sat Freddy.

"Yes, it *is* a coincidence, isn't it?" he agreed amicably, in answer to Meg's bewildered stare. "Out of all the hotels in town, I happen to have picked on the very one where your sister is staying. Extraordinary. But then, you know, coincidences tend to run in your family. I seem to remember one or two others, of which you have told me yourself."

CHAPTER VIII

For the next two days it rained; rained with a steady, drenching passion which made Meg think, for the first time in years, of the Bible story of the Flood.

"And the windows of Heaven were opened . . ." How the words conveyed the reckless, triumphant quality of rain like this! And the caravan, flimsy, overcrowded and self-contained, was just like the Ark. Except, of course, that in the Ark they didn't have to play Ludo. Not that any self-respecting aunt minds playing Ludo once, or even twice. But when it comes to playing it five—six—even seven times . . .

And through the pounding of the rain on the thin roof, and the sputtering of the over-filled saucepan on the stove, Isabel was *still* talking about her raincoat belt. If only she'd known, she explained for the third time, that they'd be going back to the hotel after all, she'd never have taken the raincoat on that walk, and then she'd never have lost the belt. But Meg had been so absolutely *positive* that they weren't going back . . .

"Oh, don't be silly. You know you'd have been frozen without it," Meg retorted, padding her counter round another of those endless zigzag bends.

Isabel didn't exactly deny this; but she managed to convey that not going back to the hotel would have made an extra reason for taking the coat; and that losing a belt for two reasons was somehow more economical than losing it for one.

"Auntie Meg! You could have caught me!"

Johnnie's voice was reproachful, not triumphant. A year ago he would have been delighted at such an oversight on the part of his opponent: now he was merely critical. "You're not playing properly, Auntie Meg."

"I'm sick of playing, that's why," explained Meg candidly. "Wouldn't you rather go for a swim?"

Why had she said that? Now Isabel would say once more:

"But it's much too wet to swim," and Johnnie, agog all over again with infantile wit, would squeal: "But, Mummy, you have to get wet if you swim!" It was like an endlessly repeated gramophone record, and this time it was Meg herself who had put it on.

"But it's much too wet——" Isabel was beginning; and for a moment Meg could have fancied that her ill-timed suggestion had stirred into clockwork life not only Isabel but the caravan itself; for it began to lurch and groan; a clumsy, thunderous movement on the steps outside set the counters shuddering on the Ludo board, and the door burst open to admit a swirl of rain, a plastic mackintosh, and a flapping surge of newspaper. This invasion resolved itself within a few moments into Mrs Hutchins, her golden curls still miraculously neat under the sheltering newspaper, and in her hand a sodden telegram.

"For you, dear," she announced, dripping exuberantly all over the tiny space as she thrust the telegram in Isabel's direction. "I ran into the chappie coming along, and I thought it would save a bit of time if I brought it along myself. My, what a day! And yesterday too! Oh my!"

There was awe in her voice as well as injury. Had she, too, felt in touch with that first drenching of mankind, ten thousand years ago? For there was this to be said for the caravans, you were truly in contact here with the primitive tyranny of weather. Not for the caravan dwellers the surreptitious enjoyment of a cosy afternoon indoors with the rain pattering companionably on the windows, pleasantly emphasising the warmth and security within. Here the rain made a different sound; a purposeful, imperious sound, as if it knew that the people here were at its mercy. Sooner or later it would find cracks and weak places in these flimsy structures, and would be able to get in. Here there was no cosiness indoors, only cramped boredom, and the feel of sodden shoes when you haven't a spare pair. Yes, here the rain was real, the discomforts were real, and as old as mankind itself.

"Not bad news, I hope?"

Mrs Hutchins was not really asking a question; she was commanding Isabel to get on and open the telegram, instead of fingering it, turning it this way and that, peering at it, like a wary purchaser testing the quality of a piece of material. After all her trouble bringing it here, Mrs Hutchins was not going to be done out of the opening of it; of the excitement, distress, or astonishment which might, even at second-hand, enliven the deadly boredom of the day. Her large body fidgeted peremptorily within its enveloping plastic.

"Yes—Oh, well, I think it's just from my husband, to say when he's coming. Or that he can't come." Isabel still fingered the telegram busily, as though the repeated imprint of her fingers might somehow alter the message inside, bring it more into line with her hopes, whatever these might be.

"Here, I'll open it." Meg seized the envelope and tore it open. "Yes, it's only Philip. He's arriving on the six o'clock train." Then, as she handed it back to her sister: "Why on earth are you looking so flabbergasted? You said it was probably that."

"I know. I'm not. I mean it's—Oh dear, just *look* at the rain! I don't know *what* Philip will say!"

She gazed at the downpour wide-eyed, and with such an idiotic air of self-reproach that Meg burst out laughing.

"He'll say you should have called in the plumber, I suppose," she teased. "Unless he's a do-it-yourself addict, and thinks you should run about catching the drops with a teaspoon. I mean—*really, Isabel!*"

But Isabel was not even listening. "And all these comics!" she went on distractedly. "And Johnnie's matchbox tops! Philip's always saying I shouldn't encourage such pointless hobbies, but I don't see how I can make Johnnie just throw them away, can I? And the shrimping nets just inside the door, but I don't know where else we can keep them. And I can't turn the sink back into a table *every* time, because as soon as you've finished washing up it's time to do the potatoes, and—"

"The particular sort, is he?" Mrs Hutchins was by now exuding sympathy from every plastic fold as she sensed a problem within the range of her experience. The caravan lurched alarmingly as she settled herself on an upturned box and continued: "My hubby was like that, particular, when he came out the Army, but it don't do to give in to them too much, you know. It's no kindness to them, not in the end it isn't, and then you've got to consider the kiddies too. Very sharp with the kiddies my hubby was, very sharp: 'Do this!—'Do that!' "—the caravan rocked again at Mrs Hutchins' idea of a parade-ground command—"Always on at them, one thing and another. The eldest one mostly, he was the trouble."

"Oh, do you find that too? Oh, I'm so glad!"

The heartless-seeming words were spoken with such a desperate fellow-feeling that no one could have taken them amiss; it was almost as if Isabel was flinging herself into her visitor's arms in her desperate need for sympathy. "It's worst of all when we're on holiday like this," Isabel continued. "Holidays are terribly difficult, don't you think, everybody on top of each other, and nothing to do?"

Mrs Hutchins nodded her head sympathetically, and with a fresh shower of drops on the cushions.

"It's a job, isn't it?" she agreed. "But it's only a fortnight, that's what I always say. You can keep going for a fortnight."

"But it's *three weeks* for us!" wailed Isabel. "And besides, it isn't just the holiday itself. It's the thinking about it before-hand. It hangs over you half the summer, getting it arranged and wondering if it's going to go off all right. And then, as soon as that's over, you have to start worrying about Christmas!" she concluded dismally.

Neither of them, Meg noticed, seemed to find anything funny about the conversation. Mrs Hutchins was nodding her head in grave acquiescence.

"It's a job, isn't it?" she repeated—her sympathy evidently more extensive than her vocabulary. "But you don't want to let it get you down. And you must make them help, you know, dear, when you're on holiday. It's no holiday for you, is it, if you got it all to do the same as at home."

"Oh, I don't mind the *work*!" declared Isabel fervently. "That's nothing. The actual work is never more than a tiny bit of running a home. No, it's the—sort of—the keeping everyone happy—not annoying each other—that kind of thing. When you're at home you have to spend half your time doing that, and when you're on holiday you have to spend *all* your time doing it. That's what's so exhausting."

Mrs Hutchins nodded again, more in sympathy than in clear understanding.

"Of course, your kiddies are still little, that's what it is," she said. "They're just like mine were when their Dad came back from overseas. You wouldn't credit it, what I had to go through. You see, Georgie—that's the oldest one—Georgie'd been only a little lad, about like your Peter, when his Dad went away, and Stevie, he wasn't there at all, he wasn't born for another six months. My hubby was gone the best part of three years, and so when he came back there was Stevie, just the same age Georgie'd been when he went away. And I reckon he felt Stevie was the kiddie he really knew—being just the same age he remembered, if you understand—while Georgie was the strange one, grown up out of all recognition.

That's how I reckon it was, because he took to Stevie at once, but he couldn't seem to get along with Georgie at all. The kiddie got on his nerves, back-answering, one thing and another. It nearly drove me barmy, I don't mind telling you. But it doesn't do to interfere, not beyond a point, though I could have knocked their two heads together sometimes with the aggravation of it. Not now, though. They're real pals now. My hubby thinks the world of Georgie."

In spite of the limited vocabulary, the clumsy inadequate repetitions, the happy ending of this story shone forth in all its sturdy triumph; the triumph of a narrow, ill-cultivated mind stretched to the very limit of its powers to meet the demands made on it for understanding, tact, and imagination; and meeting them successfully.

Could such a triumph ever be Isabel's? Isabel, with her far better equipped mind, her far broader imagination, and yet her curious lack of—what? Meg looked at her sister questioningly. Was Philip really such an ogre as Isabel's behaviour would indicate? The news of his imminent arrival seemed to have caused her not the faintest flicker of pleasure. Was this fret and hurry and anxiety the sum total of her feelings towards her husband? And did he know it? Did she even know it herself?

". . . And now we'll have to have something proper for supper!" Isabel was lamenting. "I'll have to go down to the shops again, and I suppose I'll have to take the boys too, they've been indoors all day, they'll be so fidgety by this evening if they don't get out . . . and Peter's other shoes are still soaking . . . !"

It was a good thing, as it turned out, that Meg had volunteered to go with them, for Isabel's parcels, topped by a sodden parcel of haddock, would never have balanced on the push-chair at Peter's feet all the way home. So Meg carried the shopping bag, and the parcel of haddock grew wetter and wetter, and Johnnie kept getting his feet in front of the push-chair, and Isabel kept thinking of more and more things which weren't on her list, but which she might as well get while they were here. And it all took longer than ever because of Isabel's shopping methods. She would stand with an air of infinite leisure and detachment while the assistant wrapped up her purchases, and then, at the very end, as he stood waiting for the money, she would suddenly rouse herself, as if astonished beyond measure, and plunge frantically for her purse in the depths of her handbag; frowning, peering, scrabbling, and growing more and more flustered under the assistant's impatient gaze.

What with one thing and another, it was nearly five o'clock when they reached the caravan, and Meg was able thankfully to let the haddock and its few remaining shreds of paper slump into the sink. Why the smell of the sloppy, wearisome thing should suddenly remind her of a summer afternoon in childhood, hot and still, she could not imagine; and certainly there was no time to speculate about it now, for Isabel was already working herself into a frenzy of haste and clumsiness. As the minutes ticked on, bringing Philip's arrival nearer and nearer, Meg found herself infected, against all reason, by Isabel's mounting anxiety; so much so that, when her brother-in-law actually did arrive, she experienced a moment of senseless panic, so sharp and unexpected that she scarcely knew how to greet him.

But she was curious too. Who, essentially, was this man whom Isabel had apparently cared for enough to marry barely a year ago, and who now seemed to inspire her with such terror—there was no other word for it? Hovering on the outskirts of the family reunion, Meg studied her brother-in-law with a new and critical intensity. The firm, rather tight-lipped mouth, whose severity was enhanced by the neatly clipped moustache; the wiry, muscular figure, held so uncompromisingly upright as to make him seem both taller than his medium height and younger than his fifty years. A forbidding sort of man; a man who could not be trifled with; and yet, perhaps, a man who longed to be trifled with, just now and then? This last thought occurred fleetingly to Meg as they sat down to supper, and she fancied she caught in her brother-in-law's stern glance a flicker of bewilderment at the quietness and constraint which his presence seemed to occasion.

"Well, Johnnie, have you been a good boy while I've been away? Have you been a help to your mother?"

His tone was not unfriendly, and Meg fancied he was trying, unskilfully, to make contact with the child.

"What?" said Johnnie incuriously, and apparently oblivious of the look of irritation which now crossed his stepfather's face. Yet the look might have passed, Meg fancied, as quickly as it had come, if Isabel had not noticed it and plunged with headlong tactlessness to the rescue.

"Oh yes, he's been *very* good! He's helped me a lot.

He—he—he fetches water for me," she finished lamely. "Don't you, Johnnie?"

"You haven't given me my penny for fetching it after tea," observed Johnnie, with an obtuseness almost beyond belief; and he went on munching placidly while his mother's dismay and his stepfather's disapproval met and clashed for a terrible silent moment above his head.

"Do you mean to say you expect to be *paid* for helping your mother?"

The sharpness in Philip's voice seemed to startle Johnnie rather than frighten him.

"Yes," he said simply. "But I have to remind her about it. Mummy," he continued, with indomitable perseverance, "you owe me—"

Isabel almost choked in her haste to put matters in a more becoming light.

"It isn't quite like that, Philip," she gabbled. "It's just that—that I *do* give him a penny or two now and then—for a treat—because it's holidays you know—but it's not exactly for fetching the water—I mean—"

She glanced in wild appeal towards her son. Why, oh why, her glance seemed to say, couldn't he help her to gloss over these things a little? Not by actual lying, of course, but—

"It's twopence, actually," Johnnie corrected himself. "Because you never gave me the penny for the time the jug broke. You see, it didn't break until on the way back, so I'd done all the work of it really. If it had broken on the way there, then of course I'd only have wanted a halfpenny," he conceded, with manly generosity.

Driven by Isabel's agonised looks, Meg hastily intervened with some banal questions addressed to Philip about his journey. Politeness demanded that he should take the frown from his face while he answered her, and Meg could at once feel across the table that Isabel's tension was lessening. What did it feel like, she wondered, as she struggled to keep the wearisome conversation going—what did it feel like to possess a frown of such apparently devastating potency? A frown that could reduce another human being to trembling inanity; and then, by its mere withdrawal, allow her to become human again? And what did it feel like to be the victim? And, above all, did either of them realise how uncomfortable it all was for the onlooker?

It was not until after tea that Meg realised that there would no longer be room for her to stay at the caravan. This thought, in itself, could hardly cause her much distress after the experiences of the last hour or two, but what was the alternative?

Isabel, when consulted, had clear advice to give on only two points: first, that Meg must on no account consider going back to London; second, that it would be hopeless to try and get into a hotel, they'd all be full. Having steered the problem to this point, she seemed to feel that she had done her share of the thinking, and that it was Meg's turn to take over; which Meg, in some irritation, proceeded to do.

"I know!" she exclaimed after a few moments' thought, broken only by Isabel's final contribution to the problem—namely, that it would all be easier if only it wasn't raining—"I know! The cottage. Mildred's still renting it I know, and I'm sure she won't mind my staying there. I should think she'd be quite glad to have it used. I'll ring her up and ask her."

The ten-minute walk to the telephone box through the rain rather quelled Meg's enthusiasm; and inside the box it seemed to be raining more than ever. The chilly, shut-in dampness, enclosed by rain-spattered glass on every side, gave an illusion of wetness wetter than anything outside.

And after all Mildred was not at the hotel. No, the unknown masculine voice had no idea when she would be back. Would Meg like to leave a message?

Meg hesitated. Wetness, like cold, blurs the outlines of life, makes decisions difficult. But, after all, Mildred couldn't possibly mind; asking her permission was just a formality.

"Yes, please," she said. "Could you tell her that I—that her sister Meg rang up, and that she—that I hope she won't mind, but I've nowhere else to go, and so I'll have to spend the night at her cottage."

A silly message to leave with a stranger. Apologetic— over-explanatory. The sort of message that Isabel would leave. But then, everything was so wet. Perhaps Isabel felt all the time the way other people feel when they are soaked to the skin?

With which unedifying reflection Meg collected a few of her belongings from the caravan, and set off on her walk to the cottage.

CHAPTER IX

Even the shelters were empty this evening. Meg was no longer trying to keep to the lee side of trees and buildings, nor to keep her face turned away from the rain driving in from the sea. Instead she had thrown back her plastic hood, and with head lifted to the wind was allowing the skirts of her raincoat to blow where they would. For, if you had to be wet, there was an exhilaration in being completely, unreservedly wet; to abandon yourself to the rain as to drunkenness, with never a thought of the wearisome aftermath of drying and pressing clothes and of stuffing your shoes with newspaper.

It was not really late yet, but dusk seemed to have been falling for hours, and to be falling still over the great colourless hump of the cliff-side. It was only when she turned inland, away from the wind, that Meg began to realise that it really was growing darker, and lonelier, too. These stunted hedges, dividing into squares the grey wastes of beaten-down corn, brought a sense of desolation that had been quite absent from the screaming, windswept cliffs. Meg was no longer aware of infinite wetness, but of individual trickles of water running off her hair and down her neck. She was aware, too, that she was alone in this empty, darkening countryside; and that when she reached the cottage, it too would be empty, and darker still.

It was odd, really, that you couldn't see the cottage from farther off in this bare, almost treeless landscape. The flatness of the land must be deceptive; by some trick of undulation it was impossible from this angle to see even the rough, cinder-strewn track that led past the cottage until you were almost upon it; and then there were several twists and bends before you came upon the cottage itself, set far back from the path in a shadowy tangle of garden.

The rain was slackening now, and the steady plopping of great drops from the eaves was the first sound Meg heard as she approached the tiny, dilapidated building. At her first sight of it, grey and dripping in the encroaching dusk, she could have fancied that it had stood uninhabited for the whole of the time since that ill-starred honeymoon fifteen years ago. For the weeds stood waist-high in the garden, and the front door and windows were closed with a finality as chill and forbidding as the landscape itself.

Forbidding indeed. For it was at this moment that Meg realised that she hadn't brought a key. Like a fool, she had never thought of this difficulty when she had decided so high-handedly to leave Mildred a message instead of waiting and asking her permission. Mildred presumably still had the key in her possession, three miles away through the rain and the fast-falling night; there was no way of communicating with her now.

The little rickety gate squeaked wildly, resentfully, as Meg pushed it open, and again as—she did not know quite why—she closed it carefully behind her. Then, pushing her way past the huge nettles and burdocks that almost met over the path, and discharged great sullen drops of water as she approached, Meg reached the front door.

It was locked, of course; she had known it would be. With small hope of any better success there, she now made her way round to the back of the cottage. Here, the evening seemed to have slipped another couple of rungs towards night. The shadowy chill seemed to envelope her more completely, and the drops from the eaves sounded plumper, more succulent, as they fell in great smacks on to the worn, hollowed brickwork outside the back door.

And the back door, to Meg's astonishment, simply opened at the lift of the latch, and she found herself in a dim, stone-flagged space that became almost completely dark as she closed the door behind her.

She had to open it again, unwillingly, letting in the wild wet air and the powerful, indescribable smell of a neglected garden, where the weeds grow huge and victorious as their hedgerow counterparts can never be. And now the watery light seemed almost bright, and she could see that she was in a small kitchen, over-full of buckets, zinc baths, and receptacles of all kinds, and with a huge cold stove filling the whole of one wall. On the stove, among a medley of newspapers, jam jars and enamel jugs, stood a candle congealed into its own wax, and beside it a box of matches.

The matches would strike; the candle would burn; and, somewhat reassured, Meg fixed the candle as securely as she could into an old saucer, and set off to explore the place.

Not that there was much to explore. There was only one other room downstairs, containing a much smaller, more usable looking stove, a horsehair sofa, and a number of straight-backed chairs. On a round table covered by a heavy green cloth stood an oil lamp, ready filled. When Meg had coaxed this into smoky, muttering life, the low room began to look relatively cosy, though still over-full of chairs, whose air of chilly expectancy was unnerving.

Up above there were another two rooms—the short wooden stairs seemed to lead almost straight into both of them, for there was scarcely a landing at all, both doors being made to open on to the top steps of the stairs. Opening outwards, too, as Meg discovered when she pressed the rusty latch of the right-hand door, and almost pitched herself backwards down the dim wooden steps as the door swung out towards her.

What an awkward, dangerous, arrangement! Though no doubt you got the knack of it after a day or two. Meg edged her way round the door and into the room beyond. Her candle guttered and blew out in the sudden draught; but enough watery twilight still shone through the tiny lattice window to show up the main features of the room.

And what ugly features they were! In imagining this cottage of Mildred's, Meg had pictured worm-eaten oak beams; a four-post bed; shining copper warming-pans here and there on the whitewashed walls. But this room was papered; papered with what seemed like olive green paper covered with blobs and coils of some indeterminate colour—probably pink, you couldn't quite tell in this half-light. A huge brass-ended double bed almost filled the room; and squeezed in beside it—wedged in between wall and bed so that it seemed impossible that it should ever be opened—stood a great wardrobe of yellow varnished wood, whose monumental shoddiness seemed even in this light to dominate the room.

And everything was damp, with that clammy, permanent dampness which has little to do with the season. Standing in this room, you felt that the dampness was its own, and had always been. Neither sun nor rain, neither winter nor summer, would ever lessen or increase it.

Meg found that she was shivering. Her wet clothes, which she had scarcely noticed outside in the rain, now clung to her with icy insistence, and forced her to recognise her second mistake of the evening. She had not only forgotten the key, but she had also failed to bring anything to change into except a nylon nightdress, the very thought of whose flimsy inadequacy made her shiver the more.

She wondered if there were any of Mildred's things left here. If so, they would be in the other bedroom—nothing, certainly, could be kept in that great purposeless wardrobe, trapped eternally between wall and bed, with doors that could never be opened. Stepping gingerly from the room and across the wooden stairs, now in complete darkness, Meg entered the room opposite.

This room seemed altogether more habitable than the first—drier, more recently used. A small single bed, more in keeping with the proportions of the place, stood against one wall, and some sort of rug, Meg could just see, was spread across the uneven boards. Here, no doubt, Mildred had slept; and here, with any luck, would still be some of her clothes, in that chest of drawers by the window.

Meg re-lit her candle, and, setting it down on the dimly shining mahogany, she began her search through the drawers.

How faint the light from a candle flame seems to modern eyes! How on earth, Meg wondered, did the women of olden times manage not only to identify their garments, but to put them on; to adjust them this way or that in front of scarcely distinguishable mirrors; to rejoice in their becomingness or to lament the reverse? No wonder there were all those famous beauties, about whom very old gentlemen sometimes wax nostalgic. A blemish of feature or complexion would have to be marked indeed to show up in a light like this. Perhaps it was no coincidence that the universal use of cosmetics followed so closely on the universal adoption of electric light . . .

At this point in her reflections, Meg felt rather than saw that her search was to be rewarded. In this last drawer her exploring hands no longer met the stiff, unwelcoming texture of folded curtains, nor the clammy lumpiness of those lengths of coarse lace, for no imaginable purpose, with which strange chests of drawers are so often filled. Her hands now, in the bottom drawer, met the comforting feel of woollen garments.

Yes, they were Mildred's. Kneeling down and holding the candle low over the open drawer, Meg recognised several of them. But she had better find something as old as possible. Mildred, unless she happened to be in one of her rare moods of expansive, even silly, generosity, would not readily forgive the borrowing of anything she valued.

Well, this faded yellow jumper was old enough, in all conscience! It must be years since Mildred had worn it—or that shapeless tweed skirt, either. It was surprising, really, that Mildred, usually so fussy and extravagant about her clothes, should have possessed such garments at all, let alone have brought them away with her on holiday. Still, Meg supposed, Mildred must have dug them out while at the height of her back-to-nature mood. They would really have been quite suitable to the sort of life Mildred was pretending she wanted to live.

Anyway, they were warm. Bundling herself into the dowdy, over-large garments, Meg felt warmth coming back into her limbs, and she laughed a little at the queer, droopy reflection cast back by the little spotted mirror, which could be tipped this way and that on its stand, flinging the little room and its shadowy furniture into wild, seasick slopes and angles before her eyes.

But it does not do to laugh, however softly, when you are alone. Laughter calls for answering laughter; and when there is none, it is not like silence, but more like a very special kind of sound. A sound that must be listened for, attended to, with every faculty suddenly alert.

For a moment Meg stood absolutely still, her hand clapped to her mouth, as if the idiotic, schoolgirlish gesture could recall and re-imprison the laugh which had escaped into the expectant silence.

The silence. But, of course, there wasn't any silence. There never is, when once you begin to listen as Meg was listening now. There was not a board, nor a door, in the whole place that was not faintly moving; stirring, swelling, creaking in its death-long progress through the decades towards final and utter decay. Outside the wind had fallen, but not to absolute stillness; an enveloping haze of sound, devoid of quality or definition, made Meg remember all over again the gigantic, well-nourished weeds that filled the cottage garden and grew, luxuriant and satisfied, to the very doors. And over all, yet somehow obliterating nothing, was still the sound of the slackening rain on the low roof, light and continuous, like the pattering of tiny, busy birds.

A drop of hot wax, spilling on to her wrist, roused Meg from her uncomfortable reverie. Righting the candle, which she had allowed almost to slip from its saucer as she stood, Meg determined to go downstairs to the lamplit sitting-room. There she would look for something to read—it was just one more oversight, on a par with the others, that she hadn't brought a book with her. But there would surely be something; and the companionable familiarity of the printed word *(any* printed word, no matter how dull) would soon restore her courage. Her common sense, rather; for nothing had happened, after all. What need was there for courage?

Any printed word, she had thought; but naturally she had not reckoned on the possibility that the only book she could find would be in German. Boredom she had been prepared for—would even have welcomed. To have spent the rest of the evening poring more and more drowsily over some religious essay by an unknown author of the late nineteenth century—that might have been just what she needed to soothe her nerves before going to bed. But this German book, though boring enough (so far as her half-forgotten G.C.E. standard German would take her) was somehow not soothing. The pages were yellow; the printing, strange in any case to an English eye, looked stranger still under the yellow flaring light of the lamp; and the whole book had that curious, indefinable smell of being a hundred years old.

Meg turned the pages uncomprehendingly. She soon gave up trying to puzzle out any of the sentences. Those endless, wearisome words, syllable piled on syllable until you felt the whole thing might topple over if you tried to pronounce it: that queer, ornamental lettering . . . if you half closed your eyes and let them drop out of focus, it looked like hundreds and hundreds of little people running along roads, all in straight lines, one behind the other, their steps making a crunching noise as they ran . . .

Suddenly, terrifyingly, all Meg's drowsiness was gone. She stared at the dry, innocuous volume as if it were a scorpion.

Unjustly. Unreasonably. Verbose and tedious that long-dead Teutonic author might be; but it was not his fault that Meg should suddenly, out of her half-doze, realise that printed letters, however ornate, cannot make a crunching sound.

Only footsteps could do that. Footsteps, still distant, but coming nearer along the cinder track towards the cottage.

CHAPTER X

Of all the vast and inexplicable capabilities of the human mind, perhaps the most remarkable of all is its power to encompass, in a few vivid seconds, such a variety of images and trains of thought as would take many hours to describe; and the fact that some of these coexisting thoughts may be quite incompatible, even directly contradictory to one another, only adds to the wonder of it all.

Thus in the minute or so that it took for the footsteps to reach the cottage gate, Meg had time not only to assure herself positively that they were only the footsteps of some passer-by who would tramp on anonymously into the night, but also to prepare a complete plan of action against the conflicting certainty that they would stop at the cottage gate and move up the path towards the front door. She knew which window she would address the stranger from; and in what terms. Knew, too, in another compartment of her mind, that what she must really do was to keep quite still, let him think that the cottage was empty. At the same time, of course, she knew that this would be useless, with the lamp burning, and herself probably clearly silhouetted through the cheap cretonne curtains. And, as an accompaniment to these decisions, and seeming not to conflict with them in any way, her mind was reviewing the whole story told her by Isabel—the story of Mildred, alone here as Meg was now alone, and hearing footsteps crunching their way out of the night; shuffling mysteriously round the cottage, and then crunching their way back into the darkness.

And Mildred had thought the steps were Uncle Paul's. How could she tell? *Could* one recognise a person's steps with such certainty? With the strange omnipotence of fear, Meg seemed able to hold back time itself while she pondered; and during those advancing seconds, as the steps grew louder, more purposeful, she seemed able to meditate in an almost leisurely manner the subject of the recognition of footsteps.

What was it that distinguished one footstep from another? Unbidden, like tiny hammers in her brain, footstep after footstep immediately presented itself for inspection. Freddy's footsteps first: light, quick, with a sort of bouncing, extravagant quality, as if his weight were not quite sufficient to keep him on the ground. Philip's footsteps next, brisk and heavy, fraught with purpose. Yes, and Uncle Paul's footsteps too. Across the years she could remember them still, almost birdlike in their swift delicacy as they clicked across the polished parquet floor towards the drawing-room.

Ah, but that was the point. You could recognise a footstep in its familiar setting—the polished floor it habitually traversed—the flight of steps up which it was accustomed to hasten. But could you recognise that same footstep when it sounded in unwonted places? On stony tracks along which you had never accompanied it? On grassy verges where you had never known it tread?

And now, in the brief clarity of fear, Meg found time to know that this applied not only to people's steps, but to the people themselves. The familiar person faced by an un-familiar challenge—who can know or predict his behaviour? It would have been well if, in those strange, lengthened seconds of panic, Meg had allowed herself to follow this train of thought to its conclusion; but at the time it was the footsteps that seemed so important . . . so loud . . . so near . . . And now they were stopping.

But there was no hesitating, no fumbling such as Mildred had once described. Whoever it was lifted the latch of the gate confidently in the darkness; moved along the overgrown brick path with the assurance of complete familiarity, and round to the back of the house where the door, Meg remembered, was still unlocked, might even be swinging open in the rainy evening air. Nothing now could save her from meeting the intruder face to face. She had two choices open to her. Either to cower here and wait to be discovered, or to march boldly through into the kitchen and face whatever had to be faced.

And, after all that, it was Mildred. Mildred, fumbling and fuming at the dead stove as she felt about for the candle and matches that Meg had removed earlier in the evening. Meg, holding the said candle perilously aslant in her right hand, stared dumbfounded, an extraordinary mixture of relief and disappointment struggling for precedence in her mind. A soul keyed up to imaginary feats of courage cannot but feel deflated when confronted by an unalarming and prosaic reality.

Mildred, her dark coat glistening with wet, had turned as Meg came in. For a moment neither spoke. But now, as the candle flared up and threw its light full on to Meg's face, Mildred gave a great start.

"Meg! Why are you looking like that?"

Meg, too startled herself to recollect that her half-sister (assuming she had not received the telephone message) had every reason to be startled too, could only answer, stupidly, "Like what?" Then, as Mildred went on staring, she continued: "Oh, Mildred, you did give me a fright. I'd no idea you were coming tonight, you see, and so when I heard your footsteps—"

"Footsteps?" The word seemed to have sounded on Mildred's ears in isolation, quite removed from the rest of the sentence. "What footsteps? Do you mean *he's* been here?" The horror in Mildred's face was unmistakable; but its intensity, and, in the circumstances, its silliness, struck Meg suddenly as quite disproportionately funny— the more so, perhaps, because she herself had been suffering from such similar apprehensions such a short time ago, and equally unreasonably. All her fears—her relief—her sense of anticlimax—found vent in a burst of uncontrollable laughter; in which, after a moment of baffled affront, Mildred suddenly and inexplicably joined. For half a minute, perhaps, the cold, ancient kitchen rang with their laughter, while the candle-light on the stone walls leaped and dipped with the shaking of Meg's hands. And then, slowly, even while she was still laughing, there came to Meg the realisation that this laughter was all wrong. Neither of them thought anything was funny; and Mildred's laughter was already beginning to take on the shrill, monotonous note of hysteria.

Hastily Meg controlled herself, steadied the candle, and took Mildred's arm.

"Hush, Mildred," she said. "I'm sorry, I must have startled you terribly. Come into the front room, the lamp's on in there, and I'll explain why I'm here."

Mildred allowed herself to be led through the low warped doorway into the sitting-room, and stood, blinking stupidly, in the relative brilliance of the lamplight, while Meg plunged rather precipitately into explanations.

"You see, I did ring you up, but you were out, and I had absolutely nowhere else to go——"

"You've got that lamp turned too high. It's smoking." Mildred leaned forward and began to adjust the wick, slowly and not very efficiently, with her plump, inexpert fingers. The flame lurched and gulped, then sank to a thin blue disk. Meg felt a stirring of irritation. Mildred had clearly not been listening to a word. She began all over again:

"You see, Philip's arrived, and so there's no room for me at the caravan——"

But Mildred was still laboriously fiddling with the wick, her powers of attention apparently as dim and flickering as the little flame itself. Biting her lip in annoyance, Meg gave it up and waited until the fidgety business was over; and now, with the flame burning blue and steady, and Mildred at last seated, heavily and uncomfortably, on the horsehair sofa, Meg set to work for the third time to apologise for her presence and to explain the circumstances of it in full detail. Mildred listened attentively till the very end. Then she said:

"I know. I got your message."

There are few things more annoying to a narrator than those two words "I know" greeting the end of a tale; particularly when the tale has been of considerable length and complexity and has involved the teller in some embarrassment. It is not surprising that Meg's next words were somewhat brusque:

"Why on earth didn't you say so, then? And if you knew I was here, why were you so surprised to see me when I came into the kitchen?"

"I wasn't surprised. It was just——" Mildred stopped. She leaned forward to flick at some invisible blemish on the green tablecloth. Then, suddenly, she threw up her head, her plump face strangely working, and gabbled:

"You can't stay here, Meg! You can't! Don't you understand? You're in terrible danger!"

Meg laughed; and this time her laugh was genuine. There is nothing that dispels fear so quickly as to encounter someone who is more frightened than oneself.

"Oh, don't be silly!" she scoffed. "Honestly, Mildred, you're not *still* worrying about those footsteps, are you? You know perfectly well that it must have been a tramp, or something."

Mildred, from the opposite side of the table, had to lean sideways a little to see her sister clearly past the brightness of the lamp; and the intensity of her gaze, when it met Meg's, was a little disconcerting.

"That's not what you were thinking a few minutes ago," she pointed out, with rare penetration. "When you were alone here, and you heard *my* footsteps. You thought you were in danger then. Didn't you?"

"Well——" Meg laughed, a little self-consciously. "I was a bit scared, I admit. I mean, this is a lonely sort of place. It might have been anyone."

"You didn't think it was 'anyone'. You know you didn't. You thought it was Paul."

Mildred's tone was sombre but triumphant; and Meg guessed that with the pronouncing of the fatal name Mildred's sense of melodrama was beginning to supersede her earlier genuine alarm. She sought to improve the occasion:

"Even if it *was* Paul," she pointed out, "not this time, I mean, but that night when you thought you heard his steps. Even if it was him——which is quite fantastic——he didn't *do* anything, did he? If he'd wanted to hurt you, what better chance could he have had——you alone in the cottage like that, and before your suspicions were aroused? It just proves there's nothing to worry about. And as for saying that I'm in danger too——it just shows how illogical you're being. Uncle Paul never had anything against *me*."

This time Mildred did not lean sideways to meet Meg's eyes. The brightness of the lamp was between them as she spoke:

"You're very sure of that now, aren't you? Have you always been so sure?"

Meg started.

"What on earth do you mean? Of course I've always been sure."

"Yes, I suppose you have. You've always been sure about everything, ever since you were six years old. Quite different from me. Or Isabel."

Meg could not see her sister's face through the dazzle of the lamp, but it was clear that the words were not meant as a compliment.

"Mildred—are you trying to tell me something? Or are you just being disagreeable?"

"*Me*—tell *you* something! That would be funny!"

Mildred gave a short, hard laugh, which almost at once weakened into the familiar self-pitying sob which meant that a flood of tears was imminent. "You wouldn't believe me if I did tell you," she said sulkily. "You never believe anything I say. No one does."

"Oh, come, pull yourself together, Mildred." Meg strove to speak kindly. "Tell me what's worrying you. I *will* believe you, I promise."

The rashness, the patent hollowness, of such a promise shook even Meg herself. She wondered how, having heard whatever improbable revelations Mildred was about to indulge in, she would be able to get out of it without real unkindness. It was a stupid thing to have said; but Mildred always dissolved into tears so easily that in dealing with her one was always finding oneself in this sort of situation. Meg braced herself to put on a show of credulity; braced herself too to soothe the self-dramatising distress that must now be expected; braced herself, in fact, for everything except the possibility that she would in fact find herself believing, terrifyingly and completely, the thing that Mildred was to say.

"It was you who informed on Paul," said Mildred.

"I didn't! What do you mean? You're crazy!"

Meg's protests were mechanical, and she knew it. Already the sounds, the scents of a summer afternoon long ago were swirling round her. Memory, long buried, was clutching this way and that among the hot bright shadows; and a smell—overpowering—incongruous—seemed once more to be in her nostrils; the smell of raw haddock, just fetched from the fishmonger's . . .

"I'd brought in the shopping," Mildred was relating inexorably; "I'd dumped it on the kitchen table, and you were prying about among the parcels as you always did—'What's this, Mildred?' 'What's that, Mildred?' 'Why didn't you get any biscuits, Mildred?' Oh, I can hear your little shrill voice even now! And then, suddenly: 'Look, Mildred, look! That's Uncle Paul!' A blurred, bad picture, in an old Sunday paper, all wet with the fish inside it, but *you* recognised it. *You* showed it to me. That picture of a Wanted Man in an out-of-date newspaper—it was you who found it, not me. That's how he was caught."

Meg was silent, her memory reaching, straining to its very limits. Yes, it could have been like that. The smell of the haddock in its damp parcel; the sense of bewildered, uneasy triumph at having stirred up some adult commotion that she could not understand; it all came back to her now, confused and blurred, but unmistakable. It could have happened—*had* happened—just like that.

"But—Mildred—" Meg sought for words. "I didn't know what I was doing. I was only a child—I could barely even read at the time. He—Uncle Paul—he must have known that. It was you, after all, who understood what it was; who took it to the police."

"But it was you who found it," Mildred repeated obstinately. "That's what he'll remember. It was you who found it. Oh, I'm the one who's in the greatest danger, of course—" Mildred's voice betrayed a certain satisfaction here—"I'm the one he's really after, I know that. But, don't you see, Meg, if he should come across you—especially if he came across you here, in this cottage—he wouldn't have forgotten your part in it. I know he wouldn't. That's why you mustn't stay here. I came to warn you."

Meg was recovering herself. The strange, unnerving power of childhood memory was beginning to fade, and she was able to see the episode in proportion; as something long past, finished; something no longer of significance in their lives. She tried to explain this to Mildred.

"I *do* believe you, Mildred," she said slowly. "About my share in it, I mean. I said I would believe you, and I do, honestly. But I still think the same as I did before—that it's all over and done with. I've grown from a small child into a woman. You've been married to someone else for a dozen years. And Paul, if he's still alive, and out of prison, he too will be leading an entirely new life by now, with an entirely new set of people. Why, he wouldn't even recognise you now, I don't suppose."

She moved a little on her chair so that she could watch Mildred's face. Relief? Argument? Tears? What would be her reaction?

"Why are you wearing my jumper?"

The question, at this particular juncture, was so unexpected that Meg looked, for a second, quite absurdly guilty. Then she laughed, apologised, and explained her plight; the wet and cold that had driven her to borrowing Mildred's clothes.

"Well, you *do* seem to have made yourself at home!" observed Mildred, sourly. "Couldn't you have borrowed something else?"

"Well—I chose this because it was so old," explained Meg. "I didn't think you'd like me to take any of your nice things."

"I don't like you to take *any* of my things," said Mildred ungraciously; and then, suddenly swerving back to the former topic :

"*Why* do you think he wouldn't recognise me?"

"Why—well—" Meg was suddenly embarrassed. How do you explain to your elder sister that in the last fifteen years she has grown fat; that the sparkle has gone out of her smile; that her face has begun to sag in lines of discontent and self-indulgence; that her hair, once a soft light brown, has grown coarse and brassy with too many perms, too much dyeing and bleaching.

You couldn't, of course; and yet, looking unhappily at the older woman, Meg felt as guilty and unkind as if she *had* told her all this; as if the hurtful thoughts had carried across the green lamplit table as clearly, as cruelly, as if they had been expressed aloud. Uncomfortable, full of pity, she hastened to give a new twist to the discussion.

"But, Mildred, why don't you simply go to the police and find out what actually has happened to him? You might hear that he was dead—still in prison—anything. Then you could set your mind at rest."

"The *police?*" Mildred looked distraught. "But how could I, Meg? And why should they tell me? It's not as if I really had been his wife and had a right to know. Besides—if I went to the police—and Paul found out that I'd been to the police—*again* . . ."

Meg could see all her sister's fears returning in triple force. Hurriedly she began talking, almost at random.

"Well, never mind, you're all right now anyway—I'm here with you. Let's go to bed. You'll feel quite different in the morning."

"Yes, I suppose I will."

But Mildred made no move. She sat on, staring fixedly at the green circle of light beneath the lamp as though it were a witch's ball in which all the coming events lay revealed.

CHAPTER XI

Meg did not sleep well that night. Perhaps it was the dampness of the sheets on the great bed, a dampness that the
brief loan of Mildred's hot-water bottle had done nothing
to dispel. Or perhaps it was the uncomfortable, rather
unnerving episode that had followed on the evening's
conversation.

Mildred had at first refused to go to bed at all; and
then, having at last allowed herself to be persuaded, she
had proceeded to insist on a number of complicated
preliminaries that, it began to appear, must surely keep
them both up till dawn. First, the doors must be locked;
and not only locked, but bolted and chained, though the
bolts were so stiff and the chains so mis-shapen with rust
and disuse that it was quite an engineering feat to fasten
them to Mildred's satisfaction. Then, not content with
this, Mildred went on to insist that a heavy piece of furniture should be moved in front of each; and it took Meg
twenty minutes of exhausting argument, plus a number
of cramped diagrams drawn on the edge of a yellowing
newspaper to convince her sister that since the doors
opened outwards, this precaution would be useless. Worn
out, perhaps, rather than convinced, Mildred had at last
abandoned this scheme in favour of a burglar alarm. This
took the form of three or four tin saucepan lids balanced

above the frame of the back door—which device went off with nerve-shattering efficiency every time either of them made any sudden movement in any part of the creaking little building. The lids then had to be replaced by Meg, while she simultaneously soothed Mildred's alarm. This ridiculous performance, repeated half a dozen times, succeeded in making Meg first irritable, and then almost as jumpy as Mildred herself; so that by midnight she was wide awake, cold and nervous, and very ready to welcome Mildred's suggestion that they should make a cup of tea, even though it meant lighting the stove in the front room.

Coal and wood, Mildred explained, were kept in a shed at the back; so bolt, chain and burglar alarm had to be dismantled, and Meg, bucket in hand, stepped out into the damp, fresh darkness. Meanwhile Mildred, from the candlelit safety of the kitchen, pursued her with miscellaneous and belated directions:

"Be careful; the wind will blow the candle out," she called, just after this very mishap had left Meg in darkness: and then, at the sound of a thud and an exclamation, Mildred continued: "Be careful, there's a step down." And again, at a crash of ironmongery: "Be careful, the tools are just inside the door." Finally, as Meg was feeling her way about in the complete blackness of the shed, she heard her sister's voice continuing on a different note: "Where are you, Meg? Are you still there? Oh, hurry up! Oh, watch out for those jamjars!"—this last as a crash of broken glass brought Meg's explorations to a temporary standstill. And then, just as Meg had found the shovel and could feel that blunt insecurity of a mound of coal beneath her feet, she heard a scream.

Not a very loud scream, perhaps, but coming as it did, at the very moment when her hand touched the shovel, the effect was horrifying. It was as if the shovel itself had screamed, terrified by that groping, tentative touch of a human hand in the darkness. Meg dropped it as if it was an exploding bomb, and the bucket too; and, heedless of bumps and knocks, she blundered out of the shed and towards the back door, where Mildred, her hand on her heart, was already gulping apologies.

"I—I'm sorry! It's silly—I think I'm a bit overwrought. I thought I heard a footstep on the path. Quite close."

For nearly a minute both of them stood listening. Listening intently enough to have heard the very breathing of the birds in their nests had there been real silence. But, of course, there was no silence. They were baffled, as Meg had been earlier, by the dim flurry of the night.

A footstep, or a creaking bough? The swish of trouser legs through long grass, or merely the stirring of the great teasels, restless with growth under the midnight sky?

You couldn't tell. No one could tell. You could stand here till dawn and still be none the wiser. Meg found herself shivering, her whole body tense with cold and with the effort of listening. She pulled Mildred back into the kitchen.

"You go into the front room," she said firmly, "and open up the stove—clean it out, if it needs it. I'll go back and get the coal."

Mildred obeyed, with something like the relief of a spoilt child meeting with discipline at last. Soon the tea, and the hot-water bottle, and the argument about whether or not hot-water bottles should be filled with absolutely boiling water, had made things seem almost ordinary again.

But not quite ordinary. Lying very still in the great bed (the slightest movement was liable to dispel the hardly won warmth surrounding her body), Meg thought over the events of the evening.

Nothing had happened. Nothing at all, to either of them. Mildred had imagined she had heard footsteps, but they had turned out to be non-existent. Meg had also heard footsteps, real ones, and they had turned out to be Mildred's. Whence then the panic into which they had both (Meg admitted it) worked themselves?

It was Mildred's fault, of course. Any detached observer would surely have agreed about that. Seeking a fellow-sufferer—or maybe merely wanting to jolt Meg into paying attention to the whole business—Mildred had come along with this new alarm—that Uncle Paul might be seeking revenge on Meg as well as on Mildred herself.

Meg tried to analyse the whole thing from Mildred's point of view. Here she was, an able-bodied, not unintelligent woman, leading the idle, purposeless existence of a rich man's wife. What more natural than that she should seize on imaginary alarms and excitements as the very breath of life; and, being by nature a sociable, demanding sort of person, it was equally natural that she should want to involve other people—in this case her young half-sister—in these flights of fancy.

And yet, the story of Meg's childish part in showing up Uncle Paul was true. And (Meg was struck by this for the first time) Mildred had shown a surprising degree of conviction—not to say courage—in thus rushing out through three miles of rain and darkness for the sole purpose of warning her young sister.

But, of course, it probably wasn't her sole purpose. No doubt she would have had to come some time, anyway, to fetch her belongings, and when she got Meg's telephone message she might have felt that now, when she was sure of company there, would be the best time to visit the cottage for which she had conceived—or manufactured—such horror. And maybe she had come by taxi, along the main road—obviously there must be some approach to the cottage other than over the cliffs.

Shifting her head uneasily on the high, unyielding bolster, Meg tried to see the cottage—this very room—through her sister's eyes. Here it must have been that Mildred and Paul had slept on that ill-starred honeymoon. Had Mildred, even in those first few days, begun to suspect that her "husband" was not all that she had imagined him? Had she lain here, as Meg was lying now, staring up into a darkness misty and closed in under that low ceiling; and as she lay, had she wondered what the man beside her was thinking? Had he seemed loving to her in those first days? Had he kept up the pretence of being kind and gay? Or had he already begun to show, to her alone, the insolent, self-seeking cruelty that must have been his real self?

No wonder poor Mildred had a horror of the place; perhaps of this room in particular. For it was, in any case, a horrible little room. Meg's neck and head were both aching now from being propped up so awkwardly against the huge, rigid bolster, and she sat up to peer round into the darkness.

Now that she was sitting up she found that she was, after all, more sleepy than she realised. Her head was buzzing slightly, and her wide-eyed stare into the darkness brought moving coils and spirals of deeper darkness into her eyes. The looming shape of the wardrobe seemed to stir and heave as she stared against its bulk; and some foolish, uneasy whim made her lean out of bed and try the great ugly door.

It was unlocked; but, of course, it was impossible to open it more than an inch or two against the bed. Meg peered into the crack of deeper darkness and wondered—a little morbidly at this hour of the night—what it might contain?

Really, of course, it must be old coats. Why, you could smell the dusty, uncared-for smell from here—mould, mothballs, indifference. Forgetful, at this stuporous, impractical hour, of the fact that the cottage was regularly let out to summer visitors, and was almost certainly thoroughly cleaned and turned out at the end of each season, Meg fell to musing about the imprisoned garments. Year after year they must have hung there, trapped by the great bed. Perhaps Mildred, all those years ago, lying wakeful and uneasy, had peered into the crack as Meg was doing now; her brain, perhaps, had grown drowsy as she stared, and become filled with childish fancies—skeletons—corpses—a murdered bride . . .

Poor Mildred. Meg lay back, real drowsiness stealing over her at last. "Poor Mildred—I must try to be nicer to her." With this familiar, oft-repeated resolution, she fell into a heavy sleep.

CHAPTER XII

Meg was woken by a blazing shaft of sunshine across her face, and for a moment she lay bewildered, fancying she must have been ill. Why else would she be lying in a strange bed, with the sun so high, so hot that it must be nearly noon?

Then she remembered. She was here at the cottage, and Mildred was here too. No doubt she too had overslept after their upsetting evening, for there was no sound from her room, nor from downstairs. Uneasily, Meg wondered what time it was. For it is a curious fact that, even if one is on holiday, even if one is free to sleep the twenty-four hours through at will, nevertheless, oversleeping invariably brings with it a feeling of dismay, a sense of impending disaster. The whole universe seemed pushed out of gear by this strange awakening to the noonday sun. The humming of bees already grown drowsy in the heat; the subdued, occasional chirp of birds whose morning clamour is over; the sense of breakfast irrevocably missed and lunch grotesquely inappropriate; all add up to such a feeling of alienation from ordinary life as can only be described as fear.

Meg jumped out of the great bed; and only when she was downstairs and had stirred the embers of the stove to life did she feel secure enough to think of rousing Mildred.

Mildred, of course, would be used to waking at this sort of hour and would feel no dismay—might, indeed, be annoyed at being woken so soon. Meg decided to soften the process for both of them by making a pot of tea; and finding the kettle empty, she went with it into the garden to seek the pump which Mildred had often told her was the only source of water for the cottage.

"Where are you going?"

Mildred's face, flushed and rather cross, had appeared suddenly above a tangle of foliage near the gate, where the last survivors of a once flamboyant mass of dahlias were struggling weakly for one more summer of existence before the nettles and the young, fighting elders closed over them for ever. She was dressed in a surprisingly simple—and, for her, unbecoming—cotton frock of pale yellow. Her hair was dishevelled, and she looked thoroughly put-out.

"I'm looking for the pump," called Meg, brandishing the old iron kettle explanatorily, its black, soot-encrusted curves for a moment almost taking her breath away with their beauty against the blue, hot sky and the purple willow-herb.

"The pump? It's here, of course," Mildred explained disagreeably. "I've been trying to work it for hours. I shall die if I don't get a cup of tea soon."

She motioned Meg to approach her along the narrow, overgrown path; and there at the end, set a little to one side amid a bed of vicious August nettles, stood the pump, obstinate, rusty and old. It didn't look as if it had worked for years; and Mildred was forced now to admit, sulkily, that so far as she knew it hadn't. "Drawing water from the well," of which she had so zealously boasted, appeared now to have consisted of employing a woman from the cluster of cottages by the main road to bring her buckets of water every morning. And this system had, of course, broken down today, since the woman had not known that Mildred had come back.

"Go on—*you* try," said Mildred ungraciously, her tone implying that Meg had been bombarding her with criticisms and exhortations. Obediently Meg took the handle and plied it once or twice. The dry, unresisting feel of it was unmistakable.

"Oughtn't we to—what's it called?—prime it?" suggested Meg. "You know—pour water down to start it off?"

"What's the use of saying that?" enquired Mildred, with gloomy truculence, "when there isn't any other water in the place. It *used* to work, though—long ago." Her tone had changed now; the truculence was gone. "I remember once it wouldn't start, and I—Paul—that is—we pulled up the stone . . ."

She pointed to a slab of moss-grown paving stone on the ground by the pump. "There's a sort of well underneath," she explained, "and when it gets too low, the pump won't work and you have to get it up with buckets. We could try it."

Meg gazed doubtfully at the slab of stone with the rusty metal ring let into its centre.

"It looks pretty heavy," she said; but Mildred seemed suddenly full of energy and optimism, quite unlike her usual complaining self.

"Let's try it," she repeated; and, bending down, regardless

123

of the ominous splitting sound in the seams of her yellow dress, she took a good grip on the ring. In spite of her inactive life, Mildred was still quite a strong woman, and the stone had begun to give in even before Meg had added her weight from behind. Soon, under their united efforts, it had fallen back with a thud among the nettles, and a glistening square of blackness was exuding into the sunshine the icy damp breath of underground.

Meg knelt down and peered over the edge. The water was low indeed; fifteen feet or more of dank, slimy brickwork lay between her and the dark, motionless gleam of water at the bottom. No wonder the pump hadn't worked.

"It looks terribly shallow," she announced—and her voice rang hollow and strangely nasal as she spoke into the dark shaft. "Even with a bucket, I doubt if we can get much—"

A queer uneasiness suddenly assailed her, and she edged back into the sunshine. Without warning, without any conscious preliminaries, a picture had come into her mind, a picture vivid and painful, of the young Mildred leaning over this shaft fifteen years ago; laughing, perhaps; enjoying the vicissitudes of rustic living. And beside her—or a little behind—stood a young man, dark, inscrutable, smiling. A charming picture; a picture of young love. Was it only in the light of subsequent events that it seemed so ghastly now; so fraught with danger? Or had Mildred even then, as she leaned perilously, happily, over that brink, felt a sudden doubt . . . ?

Meg became aware of the nettles stabbing into her arms as she crouched back on her heels under the noonday sun. She was breathing fast, almost as if that problematic moment of danger encountered by Mildred fifteen years ago had been encountered again, this morning.

Had Mildred felt it too? Looking up into her half-sister's face, Meg felt that she had indeed been in touch with some long-buried memory—or was it some new fear? For Mildred too was breathing fast, and had grown pale.

An unusual closeness was between them. Without argument, without explanation, they replaced the stone and returned to the cottage, waterless.

One thing at least was clear. Since a cup of tea could not be made here, and since Mildred's survival for so much as another hour was, she continued to declare, dependent on this beverage, then Mildred must return to the Sea View Hotel. And Meg, Mildred insisted, must return with her. Whether this insistence was really due to her concern for Meg's safety, or merely to her own unwillingness to walk across the cliffs alone even by daylight, Meg was not sure; but in any case Mildred's motives did not matter to her at the moment, for she had a reason of her own for complying.

The reason, she admitted to herself as she prepared to leave, was Freddy. The last she had seen of him had been three days ago, on the day of the walk with Captain Cockerill. Freddy had then been staying, inexplicably, at the Sea View Hotel. Since then, there had been neither word nor sign from him. Was he still at the hotel? Had he gone back to London? Why hadn't he come to see her at all during that long forty-eight hours of rain when he must have known that she was marooned in the caravan with Isabel and the children?

She felt, uneasily, that she knew the answer. He hadn't come because it was raining. Freddy hated discomforts. No, more than hated—disapproved of them. Only the English, he used to declare patronisingly, would endure such things.

That was all very well. But all the same, surely any man, of any nationality, if he really cared for a girl—

Well, and who had ever said he did care for Meg? Certainly not Freddy himself. In spite of the extravagant endearments in which he sometimes indulged, he was always exceedingly careful not to say anything that even the stupidest girl could possibly believe. It was silly, really, to speculate about his movements at all. He'd either turn up again or he wouldn't; there was nothing you could do about it.

Meg finished tidying her bedroom, and then stepped across the awkward little staircase to the other room to see if Mildred was ready. She found her sitting idly in front of the small, damp-spotted mirror; when Meg's face appeared suddenly beside her own, she gave a great start. Her slightly parted lips twisted in sudden dismay, and she whirled round in her chair.

"There, there, you silly!" Meg patted her shoulder soothingly. "Who on earth did you think I was? You mustn't be so jumpy—and in broad daylight, too! Come on—if we don't hurry up lunch'll be off at the hotel. And tea too, I wouldn't be surprised. I haven't a notion what the time is."

Slowly Mildred levered herself from her seat and began to wander about the room, stuffing this and that into her bag—detachedly, as if she did not care at all what she took or what she left. That was Mildred all over, thought Meg.

Lazy and careless in the extreme about her belongings until the moment came when she actually wanted to use them, and then ready to cause any amount of trouble and disturbance in order to get them fetched, found, mended, pressed or otherwise prepared for her. Her air of pre-occupation continued even to the moment of departure, when she even began absent-mindedly to put on Meg's old raincoat which was hanging behind the door. Meg firmly took it from her.

"Wake up, Mildred, do!" she expostulated. "It won't even go on you. And it would be a rotten exchange, anyway," she added, holding out admiringly the shimmering black weatherproof garment in which Mildred had arrived.

"Oh—I'm sorry. How silly of me!" Mildred laughed, nervously. "But you don't know how worried I am, Meg, really you don't. It's all very well for you to pooh-pooh other people's troubles, but if your nerves were in the state mine are in . . ."

The account of Mildred's nerves, heavily interspersed with grievances about the heartless Hubert, who had never either understood her nor given her an adequate dress allowance (a tolerable husband should, surely, do either one or the other, though it was not clear which Mildred would have preferred) brought them, tired and very hungry, to the Sea View Hotel. Lunch, as Meg had predicted, was "off"; and there followed a protracted but vigorous argument in which the Kitchen's refusal to produce anything hot was pitted against Mildred's refusal to accept anything cold; an appropriate compromise being finally reached in the form of a pot of tepid coffee and some slices of corned beef on damp, steaming plates fresh from the sink.

At the end of this repast, Mildred announced her intention of going upstairs for a rest; and it was just as Meg was about to follow her out of the deserted dining-room that Freddy appeared.

"Hullo," he said, seating himself tranquilly on the chair that Mildred had just vacated. "Sit down again, Meg, and give me some of that real Olde Englishe coffee. Why haven't you been to see me all this time?"

"Well, I like that!" Meg laughed, suddenly gay once more. "Here—take it. It gets more Olde Englishe than ever if you don't drink it at once. Why haven't you come to see *me*, if it comes to that. I bet it was because of the rain!"

"Well—of course it was!" said Freddy reproachfully. "You wouldn't expect *me* to go out in the *wet*, would you? The things women expect! You're just like my great-grandmother."

"Your great-grandmother? Why, was that the last time you went out in the rain?"

"Don't be flippant. My great-grandmother was a very stern, very imperious old lady. Listen, and I'll tell you her story. When she was a very stern, very imperious *young* lady, just like you, she had two suitors, both so charming, so handsome, that she didn't know which to choose. So one day, a day of showers and puddles, when all the trees were dripping, she went out for a walk with these two young men. And as she tripped along the lanes on her dainty little feet, with her little bustle bobbing as she went, she came to a place where there were wild roses in the hedge, and nothing would satisfy her but she should have a spray. Oh, but not one of the nearby sprays; not any of those that were easy to reach. No, she must have *that* one, high up in the hedge, the other side of the treacherous, overgrown ditch; and with her wide, innocent little eyes she looked meltingly up at the nearest of her young men.

"And the young man? What did he do in this moment of crisis? I'll tell you. He looked down at his shoes, his lovely, shiny new shoes. As soon as my great-grandmother saw the direction of his glance, and realised that the thought of spoiling his shoes was making him hesitate even for a second, she said to herself: 'He doesn't love me! I will never marry him!' and she turned her melting glance on the second young man. He, the brave fellow, never hesitated for a moment. He plunged waist-deep into the ditch; he tore his hands on the thorns, he scattered drops of water all over his fine suit, and secured her the coveted spray."

"And became your great-grandfather," finished Meg.

"No—Oh no." Freddy looked surprised. "She married the first one. Of course. What woman would want to marry a man who looked such a sight as the second poor fellow did after the whole performance? And they were very happy, too. At least, if having eleven children and dying at the age of ninety-four is your idea of happiness. Anyway, it just shows."

"Just shows what? Have some more coffee?" invited Meg.

"No, thanks. Shows? Why, it shows that girls like you and my great-grandmother should always marry a man who keeps his feet dry, and doesn't let them get away with any such pig-headed silliness. Particularly so in your case, as you haven't got an alternative young man who does plunge into ditches for you. Or have you? And do you still love him at the end of it?"

At once Meg wanted to claim a host of admirers, all queueing up to plunge into ditches on her behalf. In her mind she reviewed the half dozen or so young men who had at various times flitted into her life and out again. Suddenly, enchantingly, she realised how dull, how insipid they all seemed now that she knew Freddy. For all she cared, the whole lot of them could fall into ditches and stay there. But Freddy mustn't know this; not just yet.

"*I'd* like a young man who could get me the spray *without* messing himself up," she declared haughtily.

Freddy laughed pityingly.

"What would be the good of that?" he enquired. "Surely the whole idea is that he should be sacrificing himself for you? If he didn't get scratched and covered with mud, where would be the sacrifice? You women make a great mistake," he continued musingly, "in imagining that an unselfish, considerate sort of man makes a good husband. He doesn't. He makes a terrible husband. You see, if a man really loves his wife, he will treat her exactly as he treats himself. If he is generous with his own time and possessions, then he will be generous with hers, too, and how will she like that? If he stints himself of decent clothes and meals for some admirable reason, then (if he really loves her), he will stint her even more, for some even more admirable reason. It's only logical, isn't it? But the selfish man—Ah!—" Freddy's tone of self-congratulatory complacence here made Meg burst into giggles—"*He* is the perfect, the utterly desirable husband. Selfish, greedy, idle—as his wife, without ever needing to be greedy or selfish yourself, you will luxuriate in the proceeds of his selfishness, will guzzle the spoils of his greed. On downy cushions you will share his idleness—"

Suddenly Freddy stopped, aghast.

"I say, I haven't been proposing to you, have I?"

Meg laughed delightedly.

"Yes, I suppose you have, actually," she said. "But it's all right; you were talking so continuously that I never got a chance to say 'yes'!" and jumping up she ran, still laughing, from the room.

CHAPTER XIII

Meg wandered alone down to the beach. She had no plans for this rare, hot afternoon; and, encased in happiness, she needed none. She did not wonder whether the conversation with Freddy had been anything more than a trivial flirtation. It did not seem to matter. It was enough that it had brought her, however unreasonably, such happiness as this; had made her, at least for one golden afternoon, in love. To understand—to analyse—to predict—such coarse processes cannot be applied to so fragile a thing. Instinctively, like a tight-rope walker, she trod gently, abstractedly across the crowded sands, lest some sharp movement, some sudden call on her attention, should dislodge her from this precarious joy.

And it did, of course. A sharper movement than she had anticipated, in the form of the edge of Peter's spade, brandished with enthusiastic welcome about the level of her knees. His squeals of rapture were soon reinforced by Isabel's voice calling from somewhere among the thickets of deckchairs; and Meg realised that her wanderings had brought her inadvertently to the Place.

"Hullo, Meg. Why are you looking so solemn?"

Meg smiled to herself at her sister's greeting. Was that how great happiness made one look? And if so, could the other expressions on people's faces be equally misleading?

Isabel's expression, for instance; that anxious, self-absorbed frown that Meg's arrival had only momentarily dispelled?

"Why are *you* looking so solemn, if it comes to that?" she said lightly, settling herself on the sand by her sister's deckchair. "Is the family playing you up?"

Isabel's frown deepened.

"No—that is—it's Johnnie. Philip's taken him fishing."

"Well—how nice! I mean, isn't it?" Suddenly Meg fancied she saw daylight. "Oh, you mean they've gone out in a boat and you're afraid Johnnie will get himself drowned? He won't, you know. Philip's terribly reliable, and he's had a lot of experience sailing. You told me so yourself."

"Oh, I know. But I don't mean that." Isabel was sitting bolt upright now. She managed to look more uncomfortable in a deckchair, Meg reflected, than most people would on a dunce's stool. "I'm not afraid he'll be drowned," Isabel was continuing, "I'm afraid that he's going to look bored. After the first novelty's over, I mean. And Philip will be so terribly cross, after all the trouble he's taken to arrange it all. And do you know—" Isabel lowered her voice here, as if awed by the hideousness of the revelation she was about to make—"Do you know, I believe Johnnie's taken a comic with him! Can you *imagine* what Philip will say if he starts reading a comic just when he's showing him how to splice his line, or whatever it is—"

"I should think he'll yell at him to put it away," said Meg, unimpressed. "And Johnnie will, and that'll be the end of it. Honestly, Isabel, I think they get on much better when you're not there interfering."

She stopped, feeling that Isabel might reasonably be offended by this unsolicited criticism. Yet surely it was a kindness—even a duty—to give her a jolt occasionally—make her realise the destructive quality of her anxieties. For destructive they were, and growing daily more so—or was it just that Meg was noticing them more? Had Isabel, perhaps, always been like this?

Meg cast her mind back to Isabel's first marriage when scarcely more than a schoolgirl. There had always, Meg felt, been something a little unreal about that brief union with poor Bill—perhaps, in retrospect, it was its very brevity that made one feel like this. People had hardly stopped saying: "I just can't think of Isabel as a married woman", when they found themselves having to think of her as a widow, with two small boys to bring up. And Isabel herself neither crushed with grief nor unbecomingly resilient: only a little vague—a little unhappy—a little anxious about the future . . .

But not anxious as she was now—now when, by any ordinary standards, she had at last found security again, and a settled home. She was meeting with difficulties, of course—she was bound to—and Philip, no doubt, was proving something less than perfect as a husband and father, but all the same . . .

Meg realised that Isabel had still made no answer to her possibly ill-timed comment. Fearing that she might have caused real hurt, Meg glanced quickly up at her sister's face. She was reassured. Isabel seemed scarcely to have noticed that she had spoken. She was shading her eyes with her hand

and gazing out across the multi-coloured landscape of heads and magazines towards the anaemic remnant of the sea.

"I can't see them any more! I think they must have come back early—and that means that it hasn't gone well! Oh dear! Philip was planning to stay out till supper-time!"

"Isabel!" Meg almost took her by the shoulders and shook her. "You're impossible! Any other wife in the world would worry if her family were back *late* from a fishing trip, and here are you worrying that perhaps they'll be early! If that's all you've got to worry about, then you're a lucky woman!"

The cliché slid from Meg's tongue thoughtlessly, almost without meaning. But its effect on Isabel was surprising. She seemed to be finding in the hackneyed words something both profound and new.

"A lucky woman," she repeated slowly. "Oh, Meg, if you only knew!" She broke off. "And yet—to worry about *that* I wonder . . ."

Fear? Bewilderment? Relief? So puzzling, so contradictory were the expressions which now in quick succession smoothed and puckered Isabel's features, that Meg felt positively relieved when the familiar look of anxiety finally returned and overlaid all else.

"Oh, I've just remembered!" Isabel wailed, "I haven't brought enough tea! I thought it would be just Peter and me, but if *they're* going to be here too . . . and you as well . . . and if I go back for the other thermos someone will get our Place . . ."

"How lovely for them," said Meg unkindly. And then, with compunction: "I'll look after the Place, Isabel, while you go for the thermos. But don't bother about any tea for me. I've only just had lunch. Or I'll go and get it if you like," she added, overcome with pity as she pictured Isabel trudging joylessly through the sunshine, her eyes fixed on the ground and her mind on the time, on whether the thermos had been washed up since yesterday, and on whether the gas pressure would be high enough.

But Isabel preferred to go herself; and when she had vanished among the deckchairs, with Peter and a bucket of dead starfish trailing alongside, Meg gave a sigh of relief. She reached for one of the shapeless plastic garments with which Isabel's holidays always seemed to be festooned, bundled it up to serve as a pillow, and lay back in the sand. Lying like this, with her eyes closed, the sun hot on her face, she could forget that this was a seaside place, and remember only that it was by the sea. The voices, the shouts, the laughter—now that their source was unseen they blurred to a uniform medley of sound, as impersonal as the beating of the waves. The sand that ran warm and silky through her fingers might have been the sand of a desert island; you would never guess from the serene and ancient feel of it that it had been dug and mauled by ten thousand spades; that it had been jostled side by side with ten thousand ice-cream cartons; that chocolate wrappings and lolly sticks had found their home in it no less than prehistoric shells. Its infinite tolerance rested in Meg's fingers for a moment; trickled through them and was gone.

As time went on, she began to wish that she had not been so positive about not wanting any tea. It would put

Isabel into a terrible fuss if she changed her mind about it now. She pictured Isabel, in the caravan, anxiously counting spoonfuls, calculating quantities of water. Philip would like it strong . . . on the other hand, Johnnie would want it weak . . . Would one of them want three cups? . . . or one? . . . or none? And what about bringing extra milk? Would there still be enough for breakfast . . . ? No wonder everything Isabel did took so long.

But not as long as this, surely? Meg glanced at her watch. She had been lying here nearly an hour. Allowing ten minutes to get to the caravan, ten minutes to come back . . . surely even Isabel couldn't spend forty minutes making a thermos of tea?

But apparently she could. At this very moment Meg caught sight of her, threading her way gingerly through the deck-chairs, and carrying the thermos in both hands as cautiously as if she were competing in an egg-and-spoon race. For all her flurries, Isabel never actually did anything briskly, Meg reflected, as she watched her sister's anxious yet leisurely progress across the sand. Her personality could have been a very restful one, gentle and undemanding, if only she herself would allow it to be. There was no harm in being slow and ineffectual—these could even be lovable qualities if only you didn't keep on battling with them, apologising for them . . .

"I'm terribly sorry I've been so long," exclaimed Isabel, tripping slightly over the leg of the deckchair and dumping the thermos—hitherto carried with such care—heavily on to the sand. "But you see, Mrs Hutchins was up there—she'd got a message for you, actually, Meg, she was looking for you—anyway, we got talking, you know how it is, and so—"

"Message? What was it?" Meg's thoughts flew, with a sharp lurch of happiness, to Freddy. So he had come out to look for her. Not finding her at the caravan, he had left a message with Mrs Hutchins that she was to meet him— where?—when?

"It was from Mildred," Isabel was saying, unaware of the dizzying disappointment inflicted by her words. "She says—are you listening, Meg?—she says she's arranging for you to take over her room at the Sea View. She says you're on no account to go on staying at the cottage, it's too lonely."

"Oh." Meg was too disappointed to pay much attention to all this. "Was that all? No other message? From anyone?"

"Why—no." Isabel looked surprised. "Isn't that enough? Are you going to?"

"Going to what?" For once it was Meg who was vague and inattentive.

"Going to take over her room, of course," said Isabel. "I think it would be a good idea, you know. I was worried myself last night, thinking of you all alone up there."

"I wasn't all alone, Mildred was there," said Meg; and then, as the message at last began to register on her mind: "Do you mean Mildred's giving up her room to me and going up to the cottage herself? Because that's ridiculous. If it's too lonely for me, then it's too lonely for her—and *she's* the one who's frightened, anyway. It's absurd."

Isabel looked helpless.

"I don't think she means to do that," she said uncertainly. "Mrs Hutchins didn't say—I mean, I never thought of asking—that is, I think Mildred means to go somewhere else altogether. You see, Meg, I think she's not only frightened of the cottage now. She's frightened of her room at the hotel, too."

"Why—what on earth?" Meg stopped at the sight of Isabel's confusion.

"I oughtn't to have told you that, really, Meg. Mildred asked me not to. She said you'd just think she was being silly."

"I think she's being silly anyway," said Meg crisply. "So you might as well tell me. Especially now you've told me that much."

"Yes. I suppose I'd better," said Isabel slowly. "Perhaps you'll be able to manage her if you know all about it. You remember that fortune teller?"

"Fortune teller? Oh. Yes. That awful walk. Mildred had her fortune told while we looked at the six-headed pigs and things. Well?"

"Well—you know she said she meant to go again—to the woman's house—for a 'proper reading'? And you told her not to? Well, she *did* go. Yesterday. And the woman told her that she was going to meet a Dark Man out of the Past."

Meg laughed.

"I wonder how much prompting our Mildred gave her for that one? What happened then? Mildred asked her if the Dark Man spelt Danger, I suppose? And this miraculous woman said 'Yes'?"

"Well—yes; something like that." Isabel laughed uneasily. "But she told her something else, too—the fortune-teller woman, I mean. She told her exactly when the danger would be. Next Thursday. At seven in the morning."

"Well! My opinion of fortune-telling goes up a bit!" said Meg, smiling. "They don't usually stick their necks out with a prediction as exact as that. But I suppose she can wriggle out of it. When Mildred goes to her on Friday and complains that nothing happened, she can say it was a *spiritual* danger, and that Mildred's wonderful courage and purity overcame it while she wasn't noticing. Mildred'll love that. But why Thursday, do you suppose? Because it's early closing?"

"Oh—well—" Isabel laughed a little apologetically. "She didn't exactly *say* Thursday, not in so many words. It's just that Mildred thinks it must mean that. What she actually said was the Mildred's vibrations are for the number seven. Or aren't. Or something. Anyway, she meant that Mildred must watch out for the number seven. The seventh hour—the seventh day—that sort of thing. And Mildred has worked it out that since she was born in February, that makes August the seventh month for her. And Thursday is the seventh of August. And, you know, it was on the seventh of August that Uncle Paul was arrested. So it all sort of fits in—"

"Isabel! You almost sound as if you believe in it yourself! But you still haven't told me what it's got to do with her being frightened of her room at the Sea View. I suppose it's No. 7, is it?"

Meg had asked the question sarcastically. She was taken aback by the eagerness with which Isabel snatched at the mocking suggestion.

"Oh, is it, Meg? Do you think it might be? I was so hoping that you'd know for certain, since it was you who booked the room for her. You see, if I could only feel sure that it's only that *that* she's frightened of, and not—well—something more . . . *Was* it No. 7? Oh, Meg, *was* it?"

The intensity of Isabel's concern was disturbing; but it was also ridiculous. Meg chose to concentrate on this latter aspect, and she laughed, perhaps more scathingly than she intended.

"I daresay it was. Or No. 77, very likely, that would be better still. How thoughtful of her, in that case, to offer it to me! But I suppose my vibrations are different. Honestly, Isabel, it's all such nonsense, I'm not going to pay any attention to any of it. I'll go to the cottage tonight just as I'd planned. She's sure to change her mind before evening, anyway, and then she'd be furious to find me established in her room just when she's discovered that her vibrations are really Number Thirteen after all, and there are no other rooms half so comfortable at the price. No. I'm keeping out of it all, thank you. And now, Isabel, what about all this tea? It doesn't look as if Philip and Johnnie are coming, so let's drink the lot."

CHAPTER XIV

Meg's second night at the cottage passed much more comfortably than her first. To begin with, she had managed to arrive quite early in the evening, and before darkness had fallen she was in bed, having thus avoided altogether the uneasy flicker of candle-light. Besides this, she was alone, with her own common sense for company instead of Mildred's manufactured terrors.

It was odd how infectious they were, these fancies of Mildred's. Meg recalled the moments of suspense— no, of real, quaking fear—that she had shared with Mildred last night. And all to no purpose, for nothing had happened—nothing had ever been going to happen; it had all been in Mildred's imagination. It was as if Mildred had a special gift of dragging others with her into silliness. Look at Isabel, only this afternoon. With what portentous solemnity she had related this idiotic fortune-telling business, impressed, apparently, against her will, against her intelligence, by Mildred's monstrous gullibility.

Well, Meg at least wasn't going to be taken in by it any more. The fortune-telling was the final straw; it had rendered the whole thing farcical, as Mildred must surely see for herself any day now—had, possibly, already seen, if only her pride would allow her to admit it.

With these comfortable reflections Meg had fallen asleep in the great bed. She woke once during the night, with a vague sense that some thumping sound had disturbed her, but it was not repeated, and before she had time to frame any coherent thoughts on the matter she was asleep again. This time she slept soundly till morning.

Another fine day. Basking in the tranquil, mounting heat, the cottage no longer seemed sinister, though it was still disconcertingly dark inside—dark, and cold too, in spite of the warmth of the day. The windows were small and deep-set; only when it was near midday did fierce, improbable ribbons of sunlight stream across the two rooms facing south, while the two north rooms remained in shade unbroken for two hundred years.

But Meg did not stay in the shadows. She wandered out through the tall weeds, opening as triumphantly as any prize blossoms to the sunshine, and out on to the cinder track, already warm to her bare feet.

It was a nice little place, really it was. Meg quite enjoyed the thought of spending the remainder of the holiday here. And it was not nearly as isolated as it had seemed at first. Only a few hundred yards away ran the main road, with a little cluster of cottages alongside. It was only this odd, inconspicuous dip in the lie of the land which made the cottage seem so cut off from the rest of the world—that, and the fact that the quickest way to walk to it was not along the main road but across the deserted cliffs.

Well, not deserted on a day like this. Nowhere, in the whole of Britain, could be deserted on a fine August morning just after Bank Holiday. From where she stood, Meg could hear the shrill, irregular shouts of picnic parties making their way across the cliffs—shouts eviscerated by distance so that they seemed to convey neither joy nor distress, neither excitement nor exasperation. Just shouts, as meaningless and repetitive as the cry of the seagulls.

"Meg! Meg! I say!"

This shout was not meaningless. Meg whirled round, hurting her feet cruelly on the rough path, to meet the cheerful salutations of Freddy, who was approaching jauntily along the path from the cliffs.

"I've been sent to fetch you," he announced, dispelling in his first sentence any notion she might have cherished that he had sought her out of his own accord. "They want you. To carry bags and things. And wipe the children's faces. And fish wasps out of the jam. And help Isabel go without whatever there isn't enough of."

"Who's 'They'? And *what* do they want me for? Do try to talk plain English, Freddy." But Meg was laughing, as she rubbed the most painful of her feet.

"English! You're right! The very language to have a word for the ordeal I've been trying to describe. A Picnic. That's it. They want you for a picnic."

"Who do? Where? You'd better wait while I put my shoes on." Meg turned and led the way back to the cottage.

"I sa-ay!" Freddy was gazing raptly at the cottage, though whether in mockery or admiration was not clear. "Is it real? May I touch it?"

"You may even come inside," said Meg, throwing open the front door with a flourish. "There you are"—ushering him into the dark little room. "At least twenty chairs to choose from. Sit on whichever one you fancy while I get ready."

She ran up the steep, creaking little staircase into the bedroom, and was just rummaging under the bed for her sandals when she realised that Freddy was in the doorway.

"Do you mind?" he enquired detachedly, as he stared about him. "I thought I'd like to explore. I say—what a whopper!" He was gazing in admiration at the great wardrobe. "Now, *that's* where you should keep the family skeleton, instead of in your handbag. I should think there'd be room for a dozen in there." He had stretched himself full length across the bed now, and was peering—as probably every visitor peered—into the tantalising crack of the door.

"Moths," he diagnosed at last. "I can hear them eating. But what will the poor things do when they've finished the garments in there? How will you get a new supply in to them?"

He yawned, and for a minute lay luxuriously back against the pillows, blinking in the sharp thread of sunlight which had begun to creep past the corner of the window. Then, abruptly, he sprang to his feet.

"Come on, girl! Hurry up, they're all waiting. I'm supposed to be fetching you. Get on then: be fetched."

"*I'm* ready," declared Meg, a trifle coldly. "So if you've quite finished your inventory of the place we could start. But where to? And *who* are all waiting? You still haven't told me. Is it just Isabel and the boys?"

"Oh, Lord, no." Freddy groaned in affected dismay, but with inner relish. "Your sister Isabel is, I suppose, the crux of the affair—the hub, as you might say. She is the one who has cut the most sandwiches, worried most about the weather, and changed her mind most about where to go. But there are many others in her train. Mildred and her diminutive military admirer—or is he yours?—"

"You mean Captain Cockerill?" Meg was somewhat nettled. "He's not all that much smaller than you are. And anyway he's—"

"—Ever so much more admiring, eh?" finished Freddy provokingly. "Where was I? You shouldn't interrupt so much. Oh yes. Captain Corkscrew. And that woman. You know."

For some inexplicable reason, Meg did.

"You mean Mrs Forrester?" she supplied unhesitatingly. "The one with the boy who knows everything—Cedric?"

"That's the one," said Freddy happily. "And as I know everything too, we ought to get along famously. Come along; they said they'd go slowly on towards the Point. And slowly will be the word, if I know anything of any of them."

And, indeed, the party had not gone far by the time Meg and Freddy came in sight of them. Captain Cockerill, chivalrously laden with so many rucksacks, bags and baskets that he looked like a little tree in need of pruning, led the way, with Mrs Forrester at his side valiantly trying to get her breath enough to go on being fascinating. Following behind came Isabel, pushing Peter in his chair and carrying two floppy canvas bags. Even Captain Cockerill's gallantry had evidently not sufficed to separate Isabel and her bags. Johnnie was dragging along beside her, and even from this distance Meg could see, from the line of Isabel's head and shoulders, that she was painstakingly and at length answering some question that he had already forgotten he had asked. Last of all came Mildred, and for a moment Meg almost failed to recognise her. She had had her hair done in a new way—a short, windswept style that suited her very badly—and she was wearing low-heeled sandals which, from this distance at least, seemed to alter the whole line of her figure, making her look dumpy and old. Philip was nowhere to be seen, and Meg concluded that he must have been called away on business again. She was not sorry. The unacknowledged tension between husband and wife could be uncomfortable for everyone.

Soon after Meg and Freddy had joined them, the whole party reached the cove that Isabel had fixed on for the day's outing, and they settled down in a large untidy circle under the cliff face. Isabel seemed less harassed than usual, Meg thought, in spite of the extra work that all these sandwiches must have caused her. Perhaps getting away from the Place had done her good—or was it Freddy's presence, which always seemed to brighten her up? She was laughing with him now—something about the hard-boiled eggs; and here was Captain Cockerill leaning across them both to take one of the eggs into his hand.

"I'll show you a funny thing," he said. "You see this egg? Now, if I were to squeeze it in my hand, with all my strength, w-what do you think would happen?"

"You'd feel a sort of tingling ache in your biceps," said Freddy, evidently not pleased at the interruption. Isabel, more co-operative, replied:

"Why, it would break, of course."

Captain Cockerill beamed.

"It wouldn't, though," he declared. "Watch!"

With a great display of teeth-clenching and knuckle-whitening he gripped the egg in his fist. Nothing happened. Glowing with modest triumph, he handed it to Isabel.

"See? You try."

Isabel tried, with equally negative results.

"Fancy!" she said amiably. "You'd never believe it was so difficult. Why ever is it?"

"You could try banging it on a stone," suggested Freddy, helpfully; but Captain Cockerill ignored him.

"It's the evenness of the pressure inside, you see," he began happily. "Although an eggshell is in itself a fragile thing . . .'

The explanation had gone on for some minutes, and Meg had eaten three sandwiches, before she realised that something was missing.

"Cedric?" she said. "Where is he?" She felt that a polite voice saying, "No, it isn't" was just what was needed to round off Captain Cockerill's monologue. "Isn't he coming?" She addressed her query to Mrs Forrester, who, rather to her surprise, turned to Mildred.

"Yes—did he say anything to *you*, my dear? You saw him last. When you went back for your sun glasses?" and then, not waiting for Mildred to reply (perhaps fortunately, for

Mildred, Meg noted, was wearing her vague expression), she turned back to Meg.

"He *is* a tiresome boy! A lovely day like this, too! He said he'd follow us in just a few minutes, when he'd finished his patience game. He must have started another one. Oh dear, it is a problem, bringing up a boy without a father!" She sighed, and Meg tried to look sympathetic; but it was difficult, recalling as she did the similar sighs of Isabel as she enlarged upon the problem of bringing up a boy *with* a father.

She glanced at her sister, who was munching a sandwich and looking dreamily serene. Was she really feeling serene for once—or was it just that article she'd been reading about children and meal times? Peter was going through a phase of being "difficult" about his food, and the article had asserted with unnerving brightness that all you needed to do was to remain serene and uninterested in whether the child ate his food or not. And so, for some days now, Isabel (as often as she could remember) had been serene and uninterested at meal times; while Peter, equally serene and uninterested, had continued to leave his food.

It was nearly three o'clock when Cedric arrived, pale and composed as usual, in spite of the heat.

"Not specially," he replied to his mother's reproachful concern as to whether he wasn't terribly hungry. Further anxious enquiries elicited the information that he wasn't specially thirsty either; nor specially hot, nor specially tired. Neither had it seemed a specially long walk—"Only three and a quarter miles, you said it was five"—the whole account culminating in the information that his lateness wasn't due to anything special.

However, he condescended to accept the sandwiches that Isabel had saved for him. Unsmiling, he examined the contents of each one, and then proceeded to devour the lot with considerable appetite.

Shortly afterwards, it was announced by somebody that the boys would love a game of rounders; and since all three boys flatly refused to play, a rather attenuated version of the game was got up among the adults—all the adults, that is, except Mildred, whose youthful hair style seemed to have done little to reduce her somnolence after lunch. So she lay in the sun, her eyes half closed, talking, in the absence of other male company, to Cedric, and extracting (one could only hope) at least occasional monosyllables from him.

Captain Cockerill turned out to be dismayingly good at rounders; but it soon became apparent that his enthusiasm for hitting the ball greatly exceeded anyone else's enthusiasm for running a quarter of a mile to fetch it; and as the game petered out, Meg found herself for the first time that afternoon alone with Freddy. Isabel had gone back to Mildred and the children, and Captain Cockerill was consoling himself for the abandonment of the game by taking Mrs Forrester down to the water's edge and showing her how to play ducks and drakes. Freddy, after one disgruntled glance at Captain Cockerill's provoking skill at this pastime also, had taken Meg's arm and pulled her out of range of the display, on the pretext of taking her for a walk along the cliffs.

But it was rather a dull walk. Freddy was unusually silent; and it was not until they were returning that Meg, scouring her mind for some subject that would interest him, thought of complimenting him on the good effect he had on Isabel. She half hoped that in acknowledging the compliment he would also unwittingly answer the question she had several times asked herself—what it was that he found attractive in Isabel—Isabel who most of the time seemed so drab, so preoccupied, so careless of her appearance?

Disconcertingly, Freddy seemed to recognise at once the question behind the compliment.

"Oh, but she is fascinating, your Isabel!" he exclaimed. "She is like a darkened room—and all you need do is switch on the light. Just the woman for a lazy man like me. Switching switches is just the kind of activity that suits me."

"You seem to know where the switch is better than most," remarked Meg, steering the perilous way between disparagement of her sister and the risk of changing the subject before her question was fully answered.

"The switch? Ah!" Freddy spoke in the knowing, mysterious way that often, Meg suspected, helped him out of the tight conversational corners in which he was apt to land himself by being a little too clever. "Your sister is a worrier, you see," he went on, at a tangent. "I've always flattered myself that I'm a good influence on worriers. Or bad, of course, according to how you look at it. Because, you know, cheering up worried people is really a vice—a sort of sabotage"—Meg smiled to see how Freddy straightened his back and walked more briskly as a paradox presented itself.

"After all, you've only got to look around to see that it's the worriers who get the world's work done. What do you suppose would happen to a business whose manager didn't worry himself into a gastric ulcer? How would any laws get passed, any wars won, if politicians and generals didn't sit up all night worrying? Do you think that aeroplane over there would stay up for a single minute if the pilot wasn't worrying about it? And if the people at the factory and the testing place hadn't worried about it? Ah, yes; it's not love that makes the world go round at all, it's worry."

"Well, in that case, I can only say I'm glad to see Isabel *not* making the world go round, now and again," began Meg; but Freddy interrupted her.

"What a shocking thing to say! Isabel, above all others, needs to worry. For one thing, she's a mother, and mothers have to worry. It's part of their job, just like providing meals and arranging for diphtheria injections. The human race has only survived because mothers worry all the time, about everything. And as for Isabel in particular—" He stopped, and smiled enigmatically. They were now in sight of their own party once more.

"Is-a-bell necessary on a bicycle?" he quoted cryptically. "In your sister's case, I would say, most decidedly, Yes."

CHAPTER XV

The walk back across the cliffs seemed very long, and as the whole party straggled in single file across the grass towards Isabel's caravan, Meg wished heartily that she had slipped away back to the cottage as soon as the packing up began. But it had seemed mean to abandon Isabel at this stage, just when she might be most in need of help; and, besides, there was no food to speak of at the cottage and she hoped to find some shops still open if she returned to the town with the others.

But the return journey had proved every bit as wearying as she had anticipated. Freddy, no doubt still in his rôle of the Worriers' Friend, had allowed himself to be monopolised by Mrs Forrester, while Meg had found herself buttonholed by Mildred, who proceeded to natter at her all over again about the danger of staying at the cottage. And as they both got hotter and tireder, so, it seemed to Meg, the whole business got sillier and sillier; and she finally snapped at Mildred to such effect that Mildred fell into a fit of sulks and lagged behind altogether, while Meg marched on, cross and remorseful, and disinclined for conversation with anybody.

And now, on top of all this, Isabel had had the foolhardiness to invite the whole party to stop and have a cup of tea at the caravan before continuing their journey to the hotel. Meg could see that her sister had already repented of the invitation, issued on the crest of her precarious light-heartedness earlier in the day, but could think of no way of getting out of it; and so here they all were, filing up towards the caravan like prisoners to the scaffold, and never did executioner look less equal to his task than did Isabel, already scowling desperately over her calculations of numbers of cups and quantities of milk.

And now, here was the last straw. Sharkey. Peter, almost asleep until this moment, had suddenly woken up and precipitated himself from the push-chair all in one movement, and was now crouching by the steps demanding on behalf of Sharkey the usual tribute of synthetic terror.

"Ow," said Isabel patiently as she hurried up the steps, her soul already hovering over the gas stove: and "Ow—Oo" squeaked Captain Cockerill sportingly, as he scuttled helpfully behind. "Ow yourself!" snapped Freddy; and so, one after another, in their various ways, they all managed to satisfy Sharkey's importunate owner, until it came to Cedric.

"Say, 'Ow', Dear," urged Mrs Forrester brightly; and Meg longed for a camera to record the expression of horror, incredulity, and affronted dignity which came over Cedric's face as he realised what was expected of him.

"Go on, Dear, just to please the little boy. Of course we know you're not really frightened," continued Mrs Forrester encouragingly; and there was a moment of tense silence, broken only by Sharkey's imperious hisses, grown a little hoarse for this, his seventh victim.

And suddenly there came a scream; a scream so differ-ent from the dutiful "Ow's" that had preceded it that even Sharkey fell to the ground, limp and voiceless. For a second no one could move.

But only for a second. Then the moment relaxed. Peter—perversely—began to howl; and Mildred—for it was she who had screamed—flopped down on the caravan steps, panting and apologising.

"I'm so sorry—my nerves!" she explained, fanning herself with a wisp of chiffon. "It—I—I thought . . . I couldn't see the little chap, you see, I just saw you all crowding round—I didn't know what had happened. I'm so sorry . . . silly of me . . ."

Still gasping, she now nevertheless managed to extract a mirror from her handbag and to pat her hair to rights. Shortly afterwards she was sufficiently recovered to allow herself to be installed in a deckchair with Captain Cockerill attentive on one side and Freddy on the other. Meanwhile Meg and Isabel made the tea, while Mrs Forrester, bubbling with eagerness to help, planted herself foursquare in front of the cupboard where the crockery was kept and told them how difficult it was about Cedric.

There wasn't enough milk, of course; and even such cups as they possessed were inaccessible until Mrs Forrester should reach a point in her troubles where it wouldn't seem heartless to interrupt and ask her to move away from the cupboard. Isabel grew more and more fussed; and Meg's offer to go and borrow milk from Mrs Hutchins only made matters worse. Milk, it appeared, had already been borrowed from Mrs Hutchins once this week; and sugar too; and half a packet of detergent. True, all these articles had been returned, but all the same, Isabel couldn't face the idea of borrowing anything more.

"She'll think I'm so incompetent," she explained dolefully; and was in no way consoled by Captain Cockerill's encouraging account of a village in Tibet where cattle roamed wild in the streets and you could catch a cow and milk it whenever you pleased.

But strong, milkless tea can be refreshing. An hour later, in much better spirits, Meg was setting off with the others in the direction of the Sea View Hotel. Mildred had stopped sulking, and had even seconded—though a trifle perfunctorily—Freddy's pressing invitation to Meg to return with them to the hotel for dinner. In fact everyone seemed more cheerful now, particularly Captain Cockerill, who had, he announced, discovered a short cut to the hotel which would save them at least ten minutes.

Well, he couldn't say he hadn't been warned. First, laughingly, by the ladies; and then, gravely and at length, by Cedric, who even stopped dead in the street to draw a map illustrating conclusively the complete and absolute wrongness of Captain Cockerill's every supposition.

And, of course, Cedric was right. Half an hour later, wandering disconsolately on the outskirts of the town, they all admitted it, Captain Cockerill positively beating his breast with a mixture of gallantry, remorse, and determination to convince everyone that the whole thing was rather fun, actually.

Further wanderings brought them to an area still remote from their destination, but nevertheless recognisable: the amusement ground which they had passed through a few days earlier on that wet and windy walk.

It presented a very different aspect now, warmed into blaring vitality by the long day's sunshine, and jammed with holiday-makers. The fortune-teller's booth—Meg was relieved to note—was awaited by a queue many yards long, so there was little fear that Mildred would be tempted once again to essay her future. Nevertheless, just in case any such notion should strike her, Meg tried to get the party to quicken its pace; whereupon, to her annoyance, Captain Cockerill hung back.

"Who's for a bit of fun?" he enquired, a little wistfully; and Meg seized his arm in no uncertain fashion.

"Come on!" she said. "We'll be late for dinner as it is. Besides, we saw everything last time."

"We didn't though," protested the reluctant Captain. "They've got the Dodgems now. And the snake-juggler— that's gone, they've got the Sleeping Beauty there instead." He pointed to the tent next to the fortune-teller—almost the very spot from which Meg most wanted to distract attention.

"Come *on!*" she repeated. "It's probably the same woman, anyway. Don't you remember how sleepy she looked? They've probably just taken the snake away and put up a new label. Do let's get on. I'm starving."

Since this was very much the opinion of the rest of the company, Captain Cockerill was over-ruled. They reached the Sea View Hotel only a little late for dinner, and the first thing they encountered—indeed almost fell over—was Cedric, stretched out as usual on the floor with his patience cards. He had, he explained politely, got back in thirteen minutes, whereas they had taken an hour and a quarter by their short cut.

"'He was always right, and now he's dead right'—that's what they'll put on your tombstone, my lad," quoted Freddy; and he and Meg escaped from the room while Cedric was still explaining gravely that he wouldn't have a tombstone as he intended to be cremated.

CHAPTER XVI

It was nearly nine o'clock, but Meg still could not bring herself to leave the comfortable, brightly lit lounge of the Sea View Hotel and set off into the twilight to walk to the cottage. It occurred to her that perhaps she had been a little hasty in rejecting out of hand Mildred's offer of her own room at the hotel. After all, if Mildred really *had* meant it, and really *did* intend to find somewhere else for herself . . . ?

But she abandoned the idea at once. Mildred was always impulsive. It was most improbable that the offer represented anything more than a passing whim—by now she had probably forgotten that she had ever made it. Anyway, it was impossible to ask her about it tonight as she had gone out immediately after dinner—probably to the pictures, which would keep her out till eleven at least.

Meg leaned back in her seat, and peered behind the heavy curtains which had already been drawn across the french windows. The dusk was deepening. Even if she started now, it would be quite dark by the time she came out on to the cliff path, with two miles of solitary walking ahead of her.

But it was silly to feel nervous. And in any case, she reflected, with the comfortable arrogance of youth, something was sure to turn up. Captain Cockerill would offer to see her home. Or (dare she hope it?) Freddy would do so. Or someone with a car. Something. Meg yawned. She couldn't be bothered to worry about it just yet, anyway; and she turned her attention back to the conversation going on around her.

It was still about the fire. The electric fire that Freddy had switched on automatically before settling into his arm-chair, and that Miss Carver had as automatically switched off again as she came into the room five minutes later.

If it had been the management that had switched it off, Freddy would probably have accepted it with a shrug as one of the eccentricities of British hotel keeping (Meg some-times suspected that Freddy must have travelled very little, so certain was he that British hotels were the worst in the world). But for a fellow-guest, a supposed ally, to display such pro-management sympathies, roused him to protest.

"Hi!" he expostulated, and Miss Carver turned on him a polite but chilly smile.

"A *fire!*" she ejaculated, but still politely. "In *August!*"

Freddy didn't see the point.

"I *like* a fire," he explained. "Whether it's cold or not. It cheers things up, don't you think?"

Miss Carver didn't.

"Not in *August*," she repeated. "Not even in September. The first of October, that's the day to start fires. My dear Mother always had the fires lit on the first of October. How we used to look forward to it, we children! Coming in from our afternoon walk and finding a *fire* in the nursery!"

The old lady's eyes were bright with memory; and, glancing up, Meg had a sudden vision of a solemn little girl, her hair tied back with a big ribbon, staring entranced at the first fire of the season. But had that moment of ecstasy been dearly bought by the long chilly discipline of fireless September evenings? Or cheaply—worth every bit of it a thousand times? Meg realised, with a little shock, that she belonged to a generation that would never know.

But Miss Carver was back in the present now, her neat little feet firmly planted on the carpet of the Sea View lounge, and her eye still fixed accusingly on Freddy, though the subject of her discourse had changed.

"What I really came in for," she was saying, "was to ask if anyone, by any chance, had seen my hat box?"

Her eye held Freddy for another moment, and then roved round the room, settling a little uncertainly on Meg.

"A hat box," she repeated; and then, as if doubtful whether girls of Meg's generation could be expected to know what hats were, she elucidated: "A light circular box with a flat top. Fawn coloured. I fancy I left it in the hall. Stupid of me, of course, but if anyone *has* seen it . . . ?"

Here Mrs Forrester abandoned for a moment the unrewarding task of telling Cedric to go to bed—a task which had occupied her with few interruptions ever since dinner—and plunged eagerly into the conversation.

"*I* saw it," she declared proudly. "I'm almost sure I did— this morning. In the porch. Where they keep the deckchairs when it's raining. Only it wasn't raining this morning, of course," she added, with muddled accuracy, and an anxious glance towards the floor. But Cedric had at last obeyed her instruction—or, more likely, had finished his game—for he had already gathered up his cards and was moving with silent dignity towards the door. She continued, with notice-ably more confidence as the likelihood of contradiction vanished into the hall:

"A sort of pale brown one, was it? With 'E.C.' on the lid?"

"That's right! That's right! But in the *porch*? I'm sure I didn't leave it in the porch. Besides, it's not there now, I've just been looking."

"Well, that's where I saw it." Mrs Forrester was positive. "This morning. Just as we were setting out for the picnic." With sudden inspiration she turned on Freddy.

"*You* were with me. We started out together. Didn't you notice it too?"

Freddy shook his head. He seemed, for once, to be making no attempt to think of a witty answer; and anyway, Captain Cockerill was now adding his contribution:

"I know what must have happened," he declared, expand-ing with potential helpfulness. "Those people who left this morning—the Liverpool lot—they must have taken it by accident, with their own luggage. They had it all piled up out there, you know. If I can be of any service . . . ?"

What sort of service he could be in such a case was clear to no one, least of all to himself. Miss Carver sensibly con-centrated on the first part of his speech.

"Oh dear! Dear me! How very tiresome! However, they will no doubt have discovered their mistake by now, and will be having the box returned to me without delay."

Miss Carver's voice did not falter as she voiced this optimistic supposition. Perhaps she felt that by taking it for granted, she would somehow be able to instil into that loud-laughing, jazz-loving troop far away in Liverpool some of that punctilious courtesy which had made life run so smoothly in her own youth. She hesitated, cast one more warning look first at Freddy and then at the electric fire, and left the room.

As soon as she had gone, Meg got to her feet.

"I really must go," she announced. "I've three miles to walk, and it's getting dark."

It worked; though to Meg's disappointment it was Captain Cockerill, not Freddy, who leaped to his feet.

"My dear young lady . . . couldn't think of allowing it . . . a pleasure to escort you . . ."

Meg was about graciously to close with this offer—after all, it was better than nothing—when she became aware of Freddy at her side.

"I'm taking her," he said with finality. "It's all arranged." And pulling her by the arm he hurried her across the lounge—now that Cedric had gone to bed it was possible to do this without pitching headlong—and out into the hall.

Here he turned to her and grimaced.

"Shades of my great-grandmother!" he exclaimed. "How do you make me do it? Three *miles*! It'll kill me!"

With which prediction he proceeded to hurry her out of the hotel and along the glittering streets at a pace which soon made her protest.

"*I'm* the one who's being killed, not you!" she gasped, laughing and clinging to his arm.

He slackened his pace a little, and grinned round at her with goblin gaiety.

"I can't help it!" he cried, giving a little skip as if to illustrate his mood. "It's the moonlight. It seems to get into my blood, and makes me want to run, and run, and run to the ends of the earth. Doesn't it get into your blood, too?"

He was dragging her along at a run now, laughing, and his laughter sounded high and wild as they came out on to the open cliff. Meg felt for an odd moment that it was her weight alone, clinging to his arm, that prevented him from floating off the earth altogether.

"It might," she answered him, "if it *was* moonlight. Actually, it's the lights from the pier."

But Freddy only laughed the more; and now something of his mood began to pump through Meg's heart and lungs. She was out of breath no more; Freddy's hand, clasping hers, seemed to lift her with an enchanted lightness across the dim turf; and the turf itself was springy beneath her feet. Faster and faster they sped across the night, and the wind was in Meg's hair.

"We are the souls of two lovers who have leaped from Lover's Leap!" cried Freddy, the words flying away behind them; and Meg could only cry in answer: "We are, we are!"

But now they were in the lane leading to the cottage, and a sudden change came over them both. Or did it only come over Freddy, while Meg's mood, so closely linked with his, merely followed in his wake? She did not know; she was aware only of a sudden deflation of spirits; a sudden realisation of tiredness; a sense of caution and doubt. She wished they had not shouted so loudly, so carelessly across the empty fields. The echoes of their shouts seemed to go on . . . and on . . . and on, breaking into the silence that would have been so much wiser, so much safer a thing.

And now they were nearing the cottage, and for the first time Meg, a disembodied spirit no longer, realised the awkwardness of the situation she had created by allowing Freddy to escort her back like this. Was he expecting her to invite him in? And if so—what then? Even the most stolid and unenterprising of men, with the most honourable of intentions, might reasonably hesitate before leaving a young woman alone in so desolate a spot; and Freddy was neither stolid nor unenterprising; and God alone knew what, if any, were his intentions. Meg felt herself blushing hotly in the darkness as it occurred to her that Freddy might think she had manoeuvred the whole thing on purpose to place them both in just this situation.

But before she had formed any coherent decision as to what attitude she ought—or, indeed, wished—to adopt, the matter was taken out of her hands. For there was a light in the cottage window. Standing there at the gate, her hand already on the latch, Meg stared at the light, for a moment quite at a loss. And then, even as she stared, the light slowly and deliberately went out.

For a full minute Freddy and Meg stood side by side in the darkness, hearing only each other's breathing. Then Meg became aware that Freddy was waiting for her to speak first— to give some explanation of it all. But she had none to give; and, after all, it was Freddy who finally broke the silence.

"They've run out of shillings," he declared; and at the sympathetic gravity with which he propounded this anti-climax, Meg found her tenseness resolving into hysterical giggles.

"They can't have—it's oil," she spluttered; and then, recovering her composure: "It must be Mildred—though why on earth she should have come here tonight—let's go and see."

She pushed open the gate, and waited for Freddy to lead the way into the darkness; but he hung back.

"You go first," he said. "You know the way through this jungle better than I do." And Meg in the darkness could hear him brushing some unwelcome leaf or insect off some part of his person.

"All right. But it's just straight on, actually," said Meg, stepping boldly forward—and crashing straight into some hard, inexplicable obstacle.

"Ouch! Have you a torch? Bother!" Meg was simultaneously rubbing her shin with one hand and trying to identify the invisible object with the other.

"It's a—a sort of barrow, or something," she reported. "We'd better go round it. It doesn't matter trampling the beds—they're only weeds."

She began to push through the tangled undergrowth to the right, with Freddy close behind her. So close, indeed, that when she stopped dead, with a quick gasp of dismay, he pushed right into her. For a horrible moment she toppled, clutching at his coat; then she righted herself, stepped back, and looked again for what she thought she had seen.

Yes, she had seen it—or perhaps not seen so much as heard—sensed it; felt a sort of dank, echoing emptiness in the very air. For there in front of her lay the black, gaping hole of the well-shaft—so black in the surrounding darkness that even now she could scarcely believe in the miracle—the sixth sense—call it what you will—that had saved her.

Freddy was beside her now. He, she remembered, didn't know about the well, and in a hurried whisper—somehow it seemed necessary, after such an escape, to talk in whispers—she explained the situation to him.

"What a *fool* Mildred is!" she finished. "She must have been messing about trying to get water again—I *told* her it was impossible—and forgotten to put the stone back. No, Freddy, don't start trying to put it back in the pitch dark; you'll only break your neck. We'll go past it carefully, and warn Mildred not to come past this way till morning—not that she ever does go out after dark, she's too frightened. Come on; I'm going to give her the telling off of a lifetime; she might have killed the lot of us."

But, as it turned out, it was quite a long time before Mildred was in a fit state to be told anything. They found her cowering in the darkness of the parlour, in such a state of cringing terror that she seemed, at first, not even to recognise Meg's voice. It was not until the lamp had been relit, and both Freddy and Meg had encouraged and reassured her, that she became capable of explaining why she was here, and what it was that had terrified her so.

She had come, she explained, in a taxi, while it was still daylight, to fetch some of her things. The trouble had started when the taxi had reached the place where the track to the cottage led off from the main road. Mildred had insisted that the taxi could, and should, take her right up to the cottage; the driver had insisted that no tyres could stand it, and he would do no such thing. In the end, of course, Mildred had had to give in; but by that time the driver ("a stupid, obstinate type of man"—Mildred seemed to be more herself again) was so enraged that he refused to wait for her return, and drove off. "And good riddance, too," Mildred had thought—until she reached the cottage and realised that she had no means of summoning another taxi for her return. By this time, Mildred explained, it was growing dark, and she no longer dared to venture out even as far as the lane. So she had lit the lamp, and then simply sat there and waited, growing more and more nervous as the darkness deepened.

"And then," she finished, "I heard footsteps—*your* footsteps of course it must have been, but I didn't know that. It was silly, I know, but when I heard them stopping at the gate I just simply panicked. I put the light out so that—whoever it was—would think the cottage was empty—and—well—that's all," she finished, rather lamely.

It all sounded sufficiently silly and Mildred-like, and Meg could not help smiling a little. But all the same, silly or not, Mildred *had* had a fright, there was no doubt of that at all. Those staring eyes, those white, wobbling cheeks as the lamplight first flared up could not have been counterfeited by the best actress in the world. Meg decided forthwith not to upset her still more by reproaching her for her carelessness with the well. Tomorrow would be time enough for that—or so she thought.

CHAPTER XVII

Half an hour later, Freddy was gone. He hadn't wanted to go, but Mildred had insisted, brusquely and ungraciously, that there was no room for him. His suggestion that she should let him have her room while she shared Meg's big bed was rejected by Mildred with such a display of horror and outrage as even Meg, accustomed as she was to her half-sister's moods, could hardly account for.

So he went; with a shrug of the shoulders and a rueful smile addressed to both of them.

"Now I'll never know whether I'm good at rescuing damsels in distress, or slaying dragons, or anything," he complained. "I'd have liked to have a go—really I would. That's the only thing I've never yet done with a damsel— rescued her from distress. And I've never slain any dragons, either," he continued reminiscently. "They're usually land-ladies, you see, and I have to be nice to them. You have to, you know, if you want to play the piano all night *and* not pay your rent." With which melancholy reflection he turned away into the night, whistling light-heartedly, and seeming surprisingly sure-footed in the darkness of an unfamiliar garden.

After he had gone, it became very quiet in the lamplit room. Several books and magazines had by now found their way to the cottage, and Meg, after one or two attempts at conversation, settled down to finishing Isabel's library book. Or, rather, tried to settle down to it. But the antics of the heroine on the Riviera seemed remote and disjointed—the more so because the binding was full of sand by now, and the pages flipped over of their own volition as soon as you took your hand off them. She was disturbed, too, by the certainty that Mildred was not really reading the fashion magazine over which her head was so assiduously bent. It is a curious fact that by doing nothing in complete silence a person can cause far more disturbance than they could by practising the trombone or moving furniture about the room.

Meg forced her attention on to the story again. If only the hero's silly uncle would come in more often; and if only they wouldn't all sit round in bars fingering their glasses . . . perhaps, if she skipped a chapter—

"For goodness sake, can't you stop that noise?"

For a second Meg was flabbergasted. *Had* she been playing a trombone? Or was Mildred dreaming . . . ?

"That book of yours!" Mildred's voice was trembling. "You keep rustling the pages—it's driving me crazy!"

Meg still stared, uncomprehendingly. Then, slowly, she began to understand. Mildred, as she sat so quietly, had not exactly been doing nothing. She had been listening; listening with a terrible intensity, and every slight movement of Meg's pages had rasped intolerably across the blank canvas of the silence on which her attention was so dreadfully fixed.

She must be imagining footsteps again, out on the cinder track. And yet, something in Mildred's pose seemed to suggest that she was listening for something at closer quarters than that; something in the cottage itself . . . something in one of the upstairs rooms . . .

Meg spoke authoritatively.

"Listen, Mildred. You must pull yourself together. You're letting your nerves get the better of you. I know—we all know—that you had a bad time once; but it's all been over and done with for years now, and it's absurd to let it haunt you like this. It's this place that's upsetting you—you should never have come back here. I wish you'd gone back to the hotel with Freddy just now. Or we could have asked him to send a taxi for you."

"Gone back with him? At this time of night?" Mildred laughed harshly. "And as to a taxi—how do I know who would be driving it? Queer things can happen in taxis. And besides"—the change in Mildred's voice at this point almost made Meg laugh—"I've told you already, the taxi-drivers won't come up this lane. Like all trades people nowadays, they consider nothing but their own convenience—"

Meg welcomed the familiar tirade. Nothing could dispel Mildred's morbid fancies so effectively as a grievance. She continued in the same vein for the best part of ten minutes, progressing from taxi-drivers to dressmakers, from dressmakers to daily women, and from daily women to hotels, with special reference to the Sea View Hotel; till at last Meg grew too sleepy even to say "Did they?" and "What a shame!" and proposed going to bed.

Was this a mistake? For a moment Meg feared that all Mildred's terrors were returning with a rush at the suggestion.

But no: the sudden pallor that had passed over her face must have been just a trick of the uneven yellow glare from the lamp. For now Mildred got to her feet quite calmly, and without a word set about locking up the cottage.

She was not content merely with locking up the outside doors; she insisted, gravely, that Meg must be sure to bolt her bedroom door before getting into bed.

"Will you promise me?" she said; and Meg, half amused, half uneasy, replied, "Well, all right; but I should have thought it would be enough if you bolt *your* door. You're the one who's frightened. Bolting *my* door isn't going to keep *your* fears away."

Mildred looked at her strangely.

"You're very confident, Meg. I know it's no use warning you, but you're in danger here, in terrible danger, and each night you stay in that room the danger grows greater. Don't say I didn't tell you"—her voice was rising now to a shrill, harsh note that Meg had never heard before—"I never asked you to stay here—never wanted you to. You're doing it of your own free will, and I can't stop you. I can't! I can't!"

She turned and ran, clattering on her high heels up the short wooden stairs, and the last "I can't" merged with the staccato slam of her bedroom door.

As Meg followed, puzzled and unsure, she heard the click of the bolt across Mildred's door; and then, turning, found her own door bolted on the outside. She had never noticed before that the door even had a bolt; feeling both amused and dismayed at the absurd lengths to which Mildred's caution had taken her, she undid the bolt and pushed open the door.

The chill, motionless quality of the air struck her, as always, on entering this room; but tonight there seemed— or was it her imagination?—some indefinably different quality to it. Was it warmer? Or colder? Or was it some scent? A scent neither pleasant nor unpleasant; too faint, indeed, to describe at all, and yet different; and unspeakably alien.

Meg lit a second candle. A third. Everything was in order, the room exactly as she had left it in the morning. It even, she assured herself, seemed positively homelike on this her third night here. Only last night she had resolved not to allow herself to be upset by Mildred's foolish but curiously infectious fears, and as a result had slept soundly. All she need do was to make the same resolution again tonight; to get quickly into bed and force herself to think of something pleasant and ordinary. Resolutely to keep out of her mind all disturbing thoughts . . .

Such as the open well shaft in the darkness of the weed-choked garden. Such as Mildred's last, hysterical words tonight. Such as the dark, narrow crack in the wardrobe. And now this faint, strange scent as she entered the room. It was easy to forget this last, because now, growing drowsy, her head under the bedclothes, she noticed it no more.

It was the crack of the wardrobe door that first intruded itself into her dream. Until then, the dream had been neutral, shadowy, devoid of feeling. Merely a wandering along some dim road, for no reason and to no destination, with someone—was it Freddy?—by her side. And now, suddenly, the wardrobe was close upon her, huge like a building at the side of the road. The door, just as in real life, was ajar, and somehow, in her dream, Meg knew that she must knock on it.

The knocks made no sound, and yet Meg knew that they had been heard; so she stood and waited, first with the unsurprise, the lunatic unconcern of dreams; and then, though still nothing had happened, with a growing consciousness of fear. Even in her dream she knew that she slipped over that distinct and terrible frontier between dream and nightmare.

She had knocked, and now she was to be answered. The crack was widening, and in her dream Meg tried to close her eyes so as not to see what would be inside.

But it is useless to close one's eyes in a dream. The ghastly and superhuman powers of the sleeping mind are not dependent on the senses, and Meg knew, even before she felt the ice-cold touch across her face, that it was fingers, long and limp as rope, that were reaching through the crack towards her . . .

She awoke gasping, as if half-suffocated, her throat contorted with the effort of a soundless scream. For one second relief flooded her; sobbing, senseless gratitude at having escaped back into the real world; and then, as suddenly, the relief froze—stiffened—and she seemed to be hovering again on the brink of nightmare.

For something *had* touched her cheek. The feeling of it was with her still. Desperately she tried to grasp the fading sensation—to define it, scrutinise it—a sort of chill weal across her face—but fading now . . . shapeless . . . shadowy . . . merging already into the memory of the nightmare that was gone . . .

With an agonising effort at self-control, Meg struggled up into a sitting position and lit the candle by her bed.

The room was quiet and empty. The door, she could see even in this flickering light, was bolted, just as she had left it.

But had the wardrobe door been ajar like that when she went to sleep? Meg could not be sure. Always, so far, she had made sure it was shut before going to sleep; but perhaps tonight, in her determination to pay no attention to anything alarming, she might have omitted to do so. Or it might have come open by itself—it would not lock, and the latch was ill-fitting and insecure. The lightest touch— perhaps even a draught of air—could set it creaking open. Well, she would shut it now, anyway. That gaping line of darkness was unnerving.

She reached out her hand towards it—and stopped. Just so, in her dream, had she reached out to knock on this same door—and had been answered from within.

And it was then, as she sat with hand poised, that she heard a stirring among the hidden garments behind the door.

All pretence of self-control was gone. Meg was at the door of the bedroom, struggling with the bolt.

"Mildred! Mildred!" she screamed, all reason, all consideration swamped in panic. "Mildred! Help! Help!"

There was no answer from across the stairway; and it was now, when her shaking fingers had at last undone the bolt, that Meg discovered that her door was bolted on the outside as well.

CHAPTER XVIII

Meg did not know how long she crouched, stupid with terror, by that locked door. But slowly, as the hours or minutes passed and nothing happened, her brain began to work again; began to try and grapple with the events of the night.

But had there in fact been any events? Had she really heard any sound in the wardrobe at all? Or was it just her over-active imagination, half waking and still shadowed by nightmare? For there were no sounds now—had not been for all this time while she had been listening—listening with a strained intensity which surely would have detected so much as a fly settling.

Or a moth settling, of course. "It's moths—I can hear them eating." With a half hysterical little laugh Meg recollected Freddy's light-hearted comment—was it only yesterday morning? And was it light-hearted? Now, in the silence and the dark, the remark seemed macabre rather than funny. And he had said something else, too; something about keeping the family skeleton in the wardrobe. He had laughed as he said it in the bright morning, and Meg had laughed too; but now, remembering the long flabby fingers of her dream she could not laugh again. Instead, she switched her mind hastily to what must be the real, practical possibilities.

It could have been a mouse, of course; or some small bird that had blundered stupidly in by daylight and was now trying, in the darkness, to blunder stupidly out again. Though it was odd that either a mouse or a bird should have remained so silent after that single bout of rustling. And there was another puzzle, too. How was it that Mildred had not heard her screams? Surely she must be there, in the other room? Was it conceivable that she might have decided, belatedly, to follow Meg's advice about staying elsewhere? That she might have set off, at midnight or later, to walk across the desolate cliff back to the town? *Mildred*, who was too nervous even to walk down the garden by herself after dark?

But of course; there was a much more plausible explanation. Meg remembered the array of bottles in Mildred's room, and recalled Mildred's habit of taking sleeping pills. No doubt last night she had taken an extra large dose "to soothe her nerves". She had done this on other occasions, and Meg knew by experience that in that case no power on earth would wake her for the next ten or twelve hours.

But people who have taken heavy doses of drugs usually snore. Meg listened, uneasily. The silence was unnatural. And why, above all, was the door bolted like this on the outside? Had Mildred, in a sudden accession of senseless caution, got up and bolted it all over again during the night? But then, if she was so concerned for her young sister's safety, why had she then proceeded to drug herself so heavily that even Meg's loudest screams had failed to wake her?

Meg thought and thought; and gradually, as the uneventful minutes passed, her thoughts began to seem tiring rather than alarming. The problems, endlessly revolving, seemed now to be actually making a whirring noise in her brain, stupefying and to no purpose, like a machine into which no material is being fed. Events—fears—nightmares—all seemed equally unreal now; and afterwards Meg would have found it hard to recall just when or by what decision it was that she had abandoned her pointless vigil by the door and had crept stiffly back to bed.

When she woke again it was late. The morning blazed with cramped brilliance, like a bedside lamp, through the little deep-set square of the window. At once Meg remembered everything, with almost unnatural clarity and completeness, and she jumped out of bed determined to do what she should, of course, have done last night—that is, to force the bolted door and to go and see if Mildred was all right.

It was a real physical shock to her braced muscles to find that the door was no longer bolted. Feeling a little foolish, she stepped across the awkward top of the stairs towards Mildred's room.

Mildred's door was ajar; and the room was empty. The bed had been slept in, and there was the usual muddle of clothes, cosmetics, medicine bottles and magazines that Mildred scattered behind her wherever she went, in the confidence—usually not misplaced—that someone would tidy them up for her.

Meg did not tidy them up. But for a few minutes she searched among them, in the anxious but desultory way of one who does not know what she is looking for. A rumpled nightdress; a delicate angora cardigan dropped on the dusty floor; a clinking jumble of bottles and jars. What clue could be hoped for here?

Clue to what, anyway? To Mildred's whereabouts? Well, that was probably quite simple—she must have gone back to the hotel. One need not even postulate any startlingly early rising either—Meg had no watch with her, but from the height of the sun it could easily be eleven by now. Probably Mildred, finding Meg still asleep, had decided that she couldn't face on her own the rigours of making a cup of tea here, and had gone back to the hotel to bully them into giving her a late breakfast there.

Uneasy, not quite satisfied with this explanation, Meg turned slowly from the room, and found herself face to face with the clue.

Not exactly face to face, in the first instance; for as she came out she was, of course, looking down at the floor to make sure of her foothold on the dangerous little stairway. And it was on the top step of the stairs that she saw it—a little scattering of white fresh sawdust on the old grey wood. Her eyes darted upwards and stopped as they reached the bolt on the outside of her own door.

Yes, it was a new bolt. Shining brassily, fresh from the bustle of Woolworths, it had been newly screwed on to the old warped door.

By whom? And for what purpose? By someone who thought that Mildred slept in that room, and intended to trap her there? Or by someone—and now Meg felt an odd jerking of her kneecaps—by someone who knew very well that Mildred didn't sleep there; and that Meg did.

"You are in terrible danger . . . each night you stay in that room the danger grows greater . . ."

Mildred's words came back to Meg as she stood there. Did Mildred really know something, then? Something more than she had divulged? All this rubbish about premonitions and fortune-telling—was there, perhaps, some solid, factual basis for it all? Something definite that Mildred knew—or suspected—and yet did not dare to state in plain words?

Mildred seemed to know—or to fancy she knew—that Meg was in danger. Why? Because of Meg's childish and unwitting share in exposing Uncle Paul?

Suddenly she recalled Mildred's astonishment at meeting her, Meg, in the cottage kitchen on that first evening. And yet she couldn't really have been astonished, for it transpired later that she had known Meg would be there.

Then Meg remembered something else. That was the evening when she had got so wet, and had borrowed Mildred's old clothes. Had this caused Mildred to notice in her half-sister a sudden likeness to her own youthful self? And had she, in the same moment, realised that Paul would notice it too; might even, in his vengeful rage, forget the passage of the years and imagine that this was Mildred herself, just as he had last seen her? Feel, perhaps, as confused as Mrs Hutchins' husband had felt when confronted by his two little sons after three years' absence?

But why, if all this was in her mind, had she told Meg nothing about it? Uneasily, Meg felt that she knew the answer: Mildred was afraid that she would be laughed at for her pains; as indeed (Meg admitted remorsefully) she would have been.

Meg was overcome with contrition. It's all my fault, she told herself; I should have shown more sympathy, then she would have confided in me. I should have known that she was really frightened. I *did* know, but I thought it was silly. After all, she always *is* being silly. For the second time, Meg had to remind herself that silly people may be faced with problems for which their silliness is not to blame; that fussy, complaining people are not immune from real tragedy . . .

But the immediate thing was to find Mildred, to make sure that she was all right. Meg remembered having seen a telephone box a few hundred yards along the main road; and hastening out of the cottage, she was soon dialling the number of the Sea View Hotel.

Yes, it seemed that Mildred was there: and, yes (with some surprise in the unknown voice) yes, she was quite all right, so far as the voice knew, but she couldn't come to the telephone at the moment as she was having a bath. Would Meg like to leave a message?

"N-no—I don't think so." Meg hesitated. The relief she felt at hearing that Mildred was safe was tempered by annoyance that she should be having a bath. What a provok- ingly casual, leisurely sort of thing to be doing, in the midst of all this anxiety and tension!

Whose anxiety? Whose tension? Was it Mildred who was frightened now, or Meg? With difficulty she recalled her attention to the telephone.

"No—just tell her that—that her sister Meg telephoned, but it's not important. Tell her not to bother."

She rang off, rather hurriedly. She hoped that she had sounded sufficiently off-hand. It would be a pity if Mildred—who had presumably slept heavily and peacefully through all the disturbances of the night—should be frightened unnecessarily by anxious enquiries after her safety. Even more of a pity if they should both become a centre of excited gossip and speculation at the Sea View Hotel. She wondered, idly, who it was she had been speaking to on the telephone—a garrulous or a reticent character? It was a man, anyway, that was something, for men were supposed to be less talkative than women. Not that this had ever proved to be the case in Meg's own experience—it was on a par with the assumption that children like sweet foods better than savoury ones, or that people hate going back to work on Monday mornings. One simply has to accept these assumptions, in the teeth of all evidence, as part of one's cultural inheritance.

Anyway, it was no good worrying about it now. The sun was shining; Mildred was safe. Meg walked slowly back along the shimmering road, almost navy blue under the noonday sun; and the screech and whirr of passing cars seemed only like one more summer sound. The full glory of the sun beating down on her bare shoulders made her feel both relaxed and strong. It would be treachery—and a crabbed pedantic sort of treachery at that—to think any more about fear or trouble on a day like this.

And so it came about that Meg was not looking for trouble at all when she found it, hidden deep among the thick quiet burdocks in the cottage garden. Or perhaps it would be more accurate to say that she was not aware that she was looking for trouble. For it stands to reason that some corner of her mind must have been more than usually alert, more than usually wary, or she would never have been glancing this way and that among the silent sunlit weeds; would never have noticed among their thick pale stalks a patch of inconspicuous, ladylike fawn. Fawn canvas. Rounded—neat—with a neat leather handle . . . and with the initials "E.C." plainly visible as Meg plunged head and shoulders into the cool pungent depths of vegetation.

Miss Carver's hat box. As soon as she had dragged it clear of the foliage, Meg could feel how light it was, and knew that it was empty.

Her curiosity, and her uneasiness, no whit diminished by this certainty, Meg laid the box before her on the path, and kneeling down she tried the lock.

It was unlocked; it snapped open, lightly and efficiently, at the merest touch, and Meg raised the lid, puzzled, as she did so, more by her own mounting uneasiness than by any thoughts of why the box should be here or of what it might, after all, contain.

It contained nothing. Nothing at all. And yet, kneeling there in the sunshine, Meg seemed to feel again, all round her, the chill and darkness of last night. For all over the lining of the box she saw smears of blood.

CHAPTER XIX

"Cuckoo! Is this hide-and-seek, or what? I've been looking for you everywhere."

Freddy's face, cool and smiling, was peering round the overgrown relics of a rose arch some yards away. Had he seen Meg stuffing the hat box back among the burdocks at the first sound of his voice? If so, he could hardly be more puzzled at her secretive behaviour than she was herself. Why was she hiding the box like this? Was it just that she was startled—had not recognised his voice?

Or was it that she *had* recognised it? Had seemed, in a strange and terrible flash, to recognise the whole scene? Another face, cool and smiling, framed against another rose arch, fifteen years ago. Cool in spite of the summer heat; smiling for the last time before the fearful discovery was made . . .

The thought passed as if it had never been—or nearly. For here was Freddy—her own familiar Freddy—smiling at her, gesturing, pushing his way through the bright tangle of weeds towards her. Why, then, wasn't she calling to him, saying: "Come quickly, Freddy, look what I've found!"

But she wasn't saying this; and there was no time, now, to wonder why she wasn't. Instead she was scrambling to her feet in guilty haste; brushing down her crumpled dress; finding a suitable expression to put on her face. And when she spoke it was in a voice unnaturally bright and casual:

"Oh, hullo. So it's you. I've been doing a bit of weeding."

A desperate attempt (and in Heaven's name, why?) to explain the stooping position in which he must have first seen her. But even as she spoke, her eyes followed Freddy's quizzical gaze across the wilderness of weeds that hemmed them in on every side. In spite of her confusion she found herself laughing, for a brief moment, with him.

"After knowing me for over a month you should be better at telling lies than that," he said reproachfully, continuing his laborious way through the undergrowth, elbows raised, like a bather crossing a swimming bath at the shallow end. Meg, meanwhile, moved a little way up the path, away from the clump of burdocks.

"For one thing," he was continuing, "you should never plunge into a lie straight away like that, at the very outset of a conversation. It's clumsy. It's crude. It draws attention to the lie right from the start. No; let me show you how to do it. You first win the confidence of your victim with smiles and sweet glances—like this. Then—" here Freddy leaped over the final obstructing brambles and joined her on the path—"then you lay your arm lightly and trustingly across her—his, I mean—shoulders—like *this*; and then you start talking about something—anything—so long as it's quite remote from the thing you were planning to tell a lie about. Like the nesting habits of the Lesser Spotted Redwing. Or the irrigation problems of Southern Nigeria. Do you see? Unless, of course, you *are* going to tell me lies about the Lesser Spotted Redwing," he concluded sternly.

By this time they had reached the cottage door, and Meg shook herself free of his arm. She was still laughing, but not with him any more. It was more like laughing at some stage show. What had gone wrong between them? Was it something in her mind or in his? Was it because she had lied to him about that hat box? Or was some deeper distrust stirring . . . ?

"Are you coming in?" she asked—and she could hear, though she could not yet bring herself to analyse it, a new, unwelcoming quality in her voice. "Did you come for anything special?"

Freddy put on an expression of exaggerated hurt—or was there the tiniest suspicion of genuine hurt behind it?

"I did, actually," he said. "But it doesn't look as if I'm going to get it, does it? But I came for two other things as well. One was to tell you that your sister Isabel is crying herself into pulp. If she isn't careful she'll soon merge imperceptibly into her own basket of wet washing, and no one will ever again be able to tell which is which. Cynical though I am about all troubles other than my own, I can't help thinking that perhaps you should do something about her. The other thing I came for was to cover up that well we nearly fell into last night. I'd hate to feel it was piling up with bodies, one after another, all through our carelessness. But I see you've done it."

"But I haven't. Oh, I suppose Mildred must have remembered it when she went out this morning." Meg glanced back down the path, and noticed now for the first time that the barrow she had knocked into last night was gone. For some queer reason, she felt that she must not call her companion's attention to this, any more than to Miss Carver's hat box. Besides, there were more important things to be discussed.

"Tell me about Isabel," she said. "*Why* is she crying?"

Freddy threw out his hands in a rather unconvincing gesture of masculine helplessness.

"How would I know? What does our Isabel usually cry about? Burnt saucepans? The international situation? Incidentally, that silent suffering fellow—Philip, isn't it?—he's popped off up to town again. Would she be crying about that?"

"No, she wouldn't," said Meg decisively. She was a little surprised to find that she could not think of anything at all that Isabel would be likely to cry about. You would expect a fussy, anxious person like Isabel to be tearful, too; but she wasn't. It was as if her anxiety quickly reached a maximum beyond which it could not go. Seeing her faced by trifling set-backs, one would say that she was a feeble, cowardly sort of person; but seeing her faced by major disaster, and still behaving in exactly the same way, might one not class her as heroic—and equally misleadingly?

But this was no time for an analysis of Isabel's character. Something was going on, and Meg needed to know about it.

"Do you mean Philip's gone just for the day?" she asked. "I thought he said he wouldn't have to be away any more this holiday."

"That's what the poor fellow thought, no doubt," said Freddy pityingly. "But Fate and your sisters—a formidable combination—have decreed otherwise. In plain English"— his voice had become suddenly brusque—"he's had just about enough of this female jittering, and he's gone to find out, once and for all, what's happened to this Uncle Paul character. Whether he's alive or dead. In prison or out. Then everyone can set their mind at rest and shut up about it for good and all."

There was a silence, in the hot, still garden. The words "Uncle Paul" seemed to have dropped with a dull thud between them; and Meg was beginning, now, to guess why.

Did Freddy know what she had guessed? It was impossible to tell. His next words were light, indifferent:

"Fate has likewise decreed that I, too, must return to town today," he declared, elaborately casual. "So goodbye."

He turned away, and Meg started as if from a trance. What was this flood of feeling that engulfed her, suddenly, blindingly, without warning? Was it relief? Or terror? Or a stupefying, disproportionate sense of loss?

"Oh, don't!" she cried; and then: "No, do!" But the decision was not in her hands, for Freddy was already beyond the gate, and he did not turn at the sound of her voice.

Meg went on standing by the cottage door, and all around her the droning of the summer world went on. Bees, cars, combine-harvesters—the lot. But all she heard was Freddy's voice, cynical, caressing, and somehow not quite like an Englishman's voice. And across the years she remembered Uncle Paul's voice—cynical, caressing, and definitely foreign. In fifteen years a foreign accent would be nearly gone.

The long white hands would still be there, though; and so would the slight, wiry build and the dark eyes, mocking, and full of enchantment.

But Freddy was still young. Fifteen years ago he would have been a schoolboy. Twenty-eight was he? Thirty? He couldn't be more than thirty.

Or could he? Age sits lightly on some. Lightest of all, perhaps, on those who, like children, have never allowed responsibilities to weigh them down; neither responsibilities towards individuals nor towards society itself.

But fifteen years in prison. That would age a man. He would come out grey-haired, broken in health and spirits.

Would he? From a modern prison? With the wholesome food, the regular hours, the utter absence of responsibility? With the welfare arrangements, the recreation rooms, the concerts? What was prison life like nowadays?

Meg did not know. She fixed her mind on speculations of possible ages, taking refuge, for the moment, in the blessed impersonality of arithmetical calculation.

Fifteen years. Uncle Paul must be over forty now. Well, surely he must? How old had he been all those years ago?

Meg had no idea. He had seemed quite old to her—but then, to a small child, wouldn't any adult seem quite old? Did children notice adult ages at all, apart from instances of extreme old age, properly labelled by white hair and a stick? If only Johnnie were here she could ask him. How old do you think your teacher is? Or Auntie Mildred? Or Mrs Hutchins?

Johnnie would say: "How do you mean?" and go on sorting his matchbox tops. But it wouldn't mean that he did or didn't know how old these people were; it would only mean that he was thinking about matchbox tops. And if she pressed him, forcing his attention on to the subject, he would merely shout, without so much as raising his eyes from his task: "Mummee! How old is so-and-so?" And Isabel, from some flustered corner of the caravan, would reply: "What, dear?—not so loud—it's rude!" and would peer wildly this way and that to see if any of the neighbours were muttering, "What a badly brought-up child! . . ."

Keep to the point. Uncle Paul might have been only twenty-two or three. Younger than Mildred herself. If he was younger than Mildred she would have been unlikely to have advertised the fact. Or he might have deceived her about his age, as well as about everything else, trusting to his veneer of sophistication and experience to carry off the lie.

Twenty-two, then. That would make him thirty-seven now. Thirty-seven. No age at all, nowadays. A man can seem a mere boy at thirty-seven. Especially, of course, if he is deliberately setting out to seem a mere boy . . .

Suddenly Meg recalled a conversation of a few days ago. She, Isabel and Freddy, sitting on the caravan steps in the twilight, discussing the possibility of deceiving the world about one's age. Which side had Freddy been on? Had he seemed at all uneasy about the subject? No, it was Isabel who had been uneasy; had spoken almost with passion. Freddy had only joked about it.

Yes, but that was another thing. Freddy's jokes. His gaiety. His endless repartee. Wasn't it all a little too non-stop; now and then a little forced . . . ?

Suddenly Meg found the tears pouring down her face. Oh, but he was funny, funny! He had made her laugh so many, many times—made her laugh so much that often she could scarcely say whether it was love or laughter that lifted and sparkled within her at the very sight of him. I don't care! she cried silently to the sunshine. I don't care if he *is* Uncle Paul—I don't care whether he's a murderer or not, so long as his laughter isn't just pretence . . . !

But she did care. Any woman would care. Another scrap of conversation from that evening flashed into her mind; a conversation set against the sparkling darkness of a seaside night. Herself declaring, a little flamboyantly, the lengths to which she would go to protect a hypothetical murderer if she loved him. And what was it that Freddy had answered?

"You wouldn't, of course. When it came to the point, you'd behave like any ordinary, sensible young woman."

Thus had Freddy disposed of her protestations of imaginary loyalty to an imaginary lover. But what else had he said?

"It's pleasant—quite extraordinarily pleasant—to know that you *think* you would."

Meg's tears fell faster. Imaginary loyalty. Imaginary lovers. How easy they both were! If only Freddy never came back, then soon he would be imaginary, too, and all Meg would need to do would be to nurse an imaginary broken heart. Her imaginary loyalty would remain for ever unshaken. Some people lived their whole lives like that . . .

But not Meg. If her heart was to be broken, it must be her real heart. Better real loyalty that fails than imaginary loyalty that triumphs. She wiped her eyes and raised them, feeble with crying, towards the blinding sunlight; and still her thoughts raced on.

Freddy might be Uncle Paul, the murderer. The man who had planned to murder his wife; and then to murder Mildred; and might now be back among them planning—what?

The open well in the darkness. Freddy following behind her, clumsily pushing into her on the very brink . . . *Was* it clumsiness? And who had left the well open in the first place? Hadn't Freddy been at the cottage the previous morning— wandering around, exploring, peering unashamedly into everything while she got ready for the picnic?

Suddenly Meg could bear the sunshine no longer. She turned, scrabbling like a sightless mole through the warped doorway into the refuge of the chill and sunless room within.

For a few minutes she sat, quite vacantly, like an audience of one, on the nearest of the stiff-backed chairs that so absurdly crowded the little parlour; but presently, as no curtain rose, no story unfolded before her, she had to face again the knowledge that the story was her own; she, and she alone, must unfold it; that her cue had been called; and she did not know her part.

Presently it came to her that though she did not know what was happening, or what was going to happen, there were still one or two things that needed to be done, and that she could do, right now. She could go and see Isabel and find out what she was crying about; and then she could go and find Mildred, and discover what it was that she knew, and had not yet divulged.

It might be something trivial, of course; something quite silly, and of no concern to anyone but Mildred. And Isabel might be crying because Philip had told her that she gave the children too many fried foods. But anyway, it would be sensible to find out. It was an extraordinary relief to have something definite and sensible to do. As though she feared that the definiteness and sensibleness would evade her if she was not quick, Meg jumped up from her chair and ran up the little wooden stairs to fetch her things.

Perhaps Freddy had been here. Just now, before he met her in the garden. Roaming about, peering into things; learning the layout of the cottage . . . And yet, among these unpleasant suspicious thoughts, there came to Meg bright as crystal, incongruous as Jove's thunderbolt while you count the laundry, a stab of longing for Freddy's presence. For Freddy to make some odd, ridiculous comment on it all and set her laughing; for Freddy to peer quizzically at that little nasty new bolt, and say: "What do you keep in there—lions?"

No, he would say something wittier than that. Something like . . .

But Freddy was a murderer. Murderers can't be witty.

Can they? Can't they? Was Freddy a murderer? Wasn't he? Meg had a queer feeling—quite as silly, quite as unreasonable as any of Mildred's queer feelings—that as soon as she went into her room, she would know whether Freddy was a murderer or not.

She went in.

CHAPTER XX

Walking—running—dropping into a walk again—Meg pushed her way blindly, rudely, through the crowds on the sea front. Her eyes were fixed on the ground in front of her, and everywhere there were legs; legs of every age and shape, all bare, and all dawdling with maddening lack of purpose, impeding her progress.

Soon she would be at the Sea View Hotel. Odd, after all her plans and fears, that she should be hurrying like this to see not Isabel, not Mildred, not even Freddy himself, but Cedric.

Cedric couldn't help her much, of course; but he could tell her just one thing. A fact, of course. A simple scientific fact. One wouldn't go to Cedric for anything more complicated than a fact.

It was surprising that she could walk so fast, and steer her way so efficiently along the busy pavements, when all the time her mind was not here among the holiday crowds at all, but still alone in the cottage, re-living, over and over again, the experience of an hour ago.

She felt again the sharp, irrational expectancy with which she had pulled open the door of her room, and then the flat, bewildered feeling, so akin to disappointment, that comes when an expected shock does not materialise. For a second she had stood in the doorway, baffled, registering the sameness of everything. The narrow strip of carpetless floor; the white counterpane stretched neat and unruffled across the bed; all was exactly as she had left it.

And it was as she stood there, staring, that the streak like black treacle began flowing swiftly across the bed. Straight and smooth and soundless, it slid across the white surface, through the crack into the wardrobe, and was gone, the coverlet of the bed unmarked, undented by its passage.

Meg stumbled on the hot kerb as she remembered how the truth had come to her; not in a flash of thought, but slowly, in actual words, the words somehow seeming more awful than the fact.

"It's a snake."

And yet she had not lost her head—Meg was proud, now, to remember that. She had not screamed, nor panicked, nor rushed headlong from the cottage. She had just stepped quietly out of the room, shut and bolted the door behind her, and sat down on the stairs to think: to fix in her mind, exactly, how the creature had looked.

For it was important that the snake should prove to be a wild snake—an ordinary British species that had crawled in by accident. Crawled in of its own accord, without malice, from the tangle of weeds and heat outside.

A grass snake? But grass snakes are green—or is it brown? Anyway, not black. And they are quite small. Vipers are small too, usually—or is it always? Couldn't there be a really huge viper—overgrown, overnourished from its life among those lush, gigantic weeds?

Or an adder? What about an adder? But adders are the same as vipers, aren't they? Are they? Aren't they? Well, then, aren't there any other British snakes—quite large ones? Or that look quite large when they are moving fast? And when you are nervous, too—anything looks twice the size if you are nervous. Of course it does. Three times the size. Four times. It is only to be expected that the mind will exaggerate in such a case. Naturally it will.

Because, otherwise, someone must have put the snake there. On purpose. Knowing that it was Meg's room. Knowing that as she lay there sleeping, the snake would creep out from its lair in the wardrobe . . . long and cold . . . like the long cold fingers of her dream . . .

It *must* be an ordinary British snake. It *must* have got in by accident. She would get a policeman to come and deal with it.

No. Not a policeman. Suppose it *wasn't* a wild snake? And suppose the policeman found out that Freddy had been here . . . in and out of all the rooms . . .

It was then that she thought of Cedric. Cedric, who knew everything; Cedric who had been laying down the law about how to tame snakes and keep them as pets. Cedric would know what sort it was. Cedric must come and look at it. She would not be putting the boy in any danger—he could easily climb up to that little low upstairs window, and look through there.

But suppose the snake would not come out for identification. It might lurk in that wardrobe for hours—days—Meg knew nothing of the habits of snakes.

But Cedric would know. He would whistle at it—attract it out with raisins—something. And then, after one contemptuous glance at it, he would say something like:

"Oh, that's just the Harmless Streaky Wood Adder. They're very common in the south of England. I've seen heaps of them. You get them in Brittany, too . . ." And Meg would laugh with relief, and with happy self-depreciation, and in her gratitude she would walk all the way home with him listening to a lecture on herpetology, with special reference to identification by the discs of the vertebra . . .

Of course it would work out like that. As Meg turned into the sudden coolness of the Sea View Hotel, she felt almost elated at the prospect of putting Cedric's encyclopaedic talents to the test. Apart from anything else, it would be satisfying to see him look a little startled, for once, when she walked up to him and said: "Cedric, there's a snake crawling about on my bed . . ."

As she had anticipated, Cedric was the only guest who had defied the hot, imperious sunshine, and had stayed indoors. He lay, as usual, stretched at full length upon the carpet, surrounded by sheets of closely written paper, the sun through the wide bay window lighting up his fair straight hair to a god-like gold. He might have been a young Apollo planning out the destiny of the world.

Actually he was planning out the times and relative speeds of all the local bus services, checking them against the timetable that lay in a blaze of sunshine a few inches from his nose.

"Did you know," he greeted Meg, without turning his head, "that you can get to Lindal Bay four minutes quicker if you don't go by the direct route? You should go on the Blue Star coach to Mortley, and then—"

"Cedric—I want to speak to you," said Meg hastily, and with a nervous glance into the hall behind. "I need your help with something that I—I—" She closed the door into the hall and came closer. "Are you listening, Cedric? I'd be awfully grateful if you didn't tell anyone else—I've come to you because you seem to know such a lot about everything—"

"Chorley 5.54. Bindon Gap 6.12. That's 7.3 miles in 18 minutes, which makes—"

All right. Let him have it. A shock would do him good.

"Cedric, there's a great snake in my bedroom up at the cottage."

It worked. Cedric stopped writing, and curled round to look up at her.

"Yes, I know," he said. "Medium-sized, actually. They can be as much as eight feet long."

"You *know*? How on earth—? I mean—"

"It's mine," explained Cedric patiently. "It's my cobra. You haven't let it out, have you?" he added, some flicker of concern at last crossing his calm features.

"No—in fact I've locked it in," returned Meg, with some asperity. "What do you mean, it's your cobra? And *why* are you keeping it in my cottage?"

"It's not your cottage," Cedric pointed out without heat. "It's Mrs What's-her-name's. Your sister, isn't she?

Actually, I thought you'd both left it. I thought it was empty, or I'd never have put Lady Clorinda there. But it doesn't matter, so long as you shut the door firmly each time you go in or out. And leave the wardrobe ajar, so that she has a dark place to go to when she wants to sleep. You didn't feed her, by any chance, did you? She should have small birds, really, or mice; but raw meat is all right. I've been giving her steak."

"Well, I *haven't*," said Meg, with some heat. "And I haven't been crawling about in the wainscoting catching mice for her, either, in case you were wondering. Honestly, Cedric, I think it's going a bit far—calmly planting snakes in other people's houses!"

"Well, I couldn't keep her here, could I?" Cedric pointed out reasonably. "I mean—my mother. The maids. There'd have been an awful fuss."

"There's going to be an awful fuss anyway," Meg declared with conviction. "And I'm the one who's going to make it. Where did you get hold of the thing, anyway?"

"Lady Clorinda? Oh, I got her from that snake-charmer woman," explained Cedric. "You know—you were there. When we went for that walk. Didn't you notice how fed up the woman looked, just sitting there, with Lady Clorinda beside her, as if she wasn't enjoying it one bit? So it occurred to me afterwards that, if she was as fed up as she looked, she might be willing to sell the cobra. So I went to see her yesterday; and it turned out I was quite right—"

"You don't say!" interrupted Meg bitterly; but Cedric went on, unabashed:

"It seemed that she'd had a row with her boss, and was on the point of walking out on the job, so when I came along with a fair offer for Lady Clorinda, she jumped at the idea. I paid her forty-five shillings. I *told* you a cobra cost forty-five shillings, and it turns out I was right," he finished, with modest infallibility.

"Not necessarily," retorted Meg argumentatively—she couldn't help herself, although she knew there were far more important things still to discuss during this brief chance of talking to Cedric privately. "It doesn't prove anything. If she wanted to get rid of the snake, she'd have counted anything a bargain. I mean, if you don't want a snake you very much don't want it, I should think. Besides, it probably wasn't hers; it probably belonged to the boss she'd had a row with. It didn't matter to her whether it was a fair price or not, since it wasn't her property."

"It was a perfectly fair price," said Cedric coldly; and Meg hastily abandoned the argument before he should waste more valuable minutes on proving his point.

"Well, you can't keep it in our cottage, anyway," she said firmly. "You must fetch it away at once. It was a frightfully dangerous thing to do. I wouldn't be surprised if you could be sent to prison for it."

"I'm under age," Cedric pointed out civilly. "And anyway, it isn't dangerous at all. Lady Clorinda's very tame. She would never dream of attacking you so long as you don't annoy her."

"If you think I'm going to devote the rest of my holiday to not annoying cobras—"

"No—I didn't mean that. I'll take her away at once, of course, if you really want me to." Cedric sounded polite but aggrieved. "But, you see, it means I'll have to keep her in her box the whole time till I go home. That room was just right for her. Plenty of room to move about, and the wardrobe to hide away in and feel safe. They like a hidden-away place like that with a narrow entrance, you know."

"I daresay they do! And *I* like a bedroom where I'm not risking my life every time I move! I'm funny that way. Really, Cedric, I hate to tell tales, but I really think I'll have to tell your mother about all this, if you don't. For your own sake, I mean, not mine. I know you think you're infallible, but you're not. Sooner or later you'll get bitten, and then you'll die. Or someone else will. You just can't do this sort of thing. I *must* tell."

Cedric seemed, for once, a little shaken.

"Oh, please don't do that!" he pleaded. "I'll come and fetch her at once. Really. And—" the admission came hesitantly, unwillingly—"actually—it's a great pity of course, but it can't be helped—actually she's not poisonous. Her fangs have been drawn. So there's no need to tell my mother, or—or anybody, is there?"

Meg hesitated. This did put the thing in rather a different light.

"Well—we'll see," she conceded. "But anyway, do for goodness' sake find somewhere else to keep it. And quickly. Poisonous or not poisonous, I just can't *imagine* what my sister would do if she saw it. She'd have a heart attack on the spot, I should think."

"But——" Cedric was beginning all over again: but at that moment the door opened, and a fair, flurried head peered round.

"Oh, there you are, Dear! I've been looking for you everywhere! Fancy being indoors on a day like this!"

Wonderful how Mrs Forrester managed to be genuinely surprised about it, every time.

Cedric gave a hunted glance at the golden radiance blazing so tiresomely outside. Then he shrugged. What with his mother, the sunshine, and people not appreciating cobras—a fellow knew when he was licked. He shoved his papers into an untidy pile, and got to his feet.

"All right," he said to his mother, resignedly; and then, nonchalantly, to Meg: "I'll get those things you asked about right away."

Mrs Forrester's blue eyes darted with pathetic eagerness from one to the other of them.

"So my Cedric is doing some little errand for you? I'm so glad. I've always taught him to be helpful," she exclaimed, trying forlornly to claim for herself some shreds of the credit that seemed, by some incomprehensible accident, to have attached to Cedric's behaviour. "I'm sure it will be a great pleasure to him to help in any little way he can. Is it some shopping you are doing for our friend, Dear?"

"*Yes*," lied Cedric boldly; and with a glance at Meg, half beseeching and half defiant, he strode out of the room.

But Meg was no more anxious to expose his lie than he was himself.

For the cobra business wasn't really explained away.

How silly she had been—how unforgivably stupid—not to have asked Cedric, while she still had the chance, the most important question of all.

CHAPTER XXI

"But I still don't understand why you're *crying* about it."

Meg had lodged this protest three times now, but had still failed to extract from Isabel any satisfactory explanation.

"It's silly, I know—I just can't help it," gulped Isabel for the third time; and then: "You don't understand, Meg."

"That's just what I'm saying," Meg pointed out patiently. "I don't understand. That's why I want you to explain. All you've told me so far is that Philip's gone up to town to find out officially what's happened to Uncle Paul, and I don't see anything in that for *you* to cry about. I expect he'll find out that Uncle Paul is still in prison." (Was it Isabel she was trying to reassure, or herself? Whichever it was, she could hear her own voice becoming more and more arrogantly confident as she continued.) "Or else dead. Or dogged by psychiatric welfare workers while he makes good at a job they've found for him in a lamp-shade factory in Leeds. So do cheer up, Isabel. Let's tidy up the caravan, it looks terrible. You'll feel better when everything's straight."

"But I feel better *now!*" sobbed Isabel disconcertingly. "I feel better than I have for weeks, for months. It's the relief of it—that's why I can't stop crying."

"Now, Isabel." Meg put her arm round her sister protectively. "Start at the beginning. Better than what? Which weeks and months? Relief from what?——No, run away, Johnnie, we're still busy. Look, here's threepence; go and buy yourself an ice cream. Don't go to the little place here, though, go to that kiosk right along the parade near the pier. You get bigger ones there," she lied unashamedly as she handed her nephew the money, rapidly calculating the number of minutes they could hope to be rid of him.

"How much bigger?" For a moment Johnnie's rival calculations met hers head on: the issue swayed in the balance.

"Huge ones. And you can get Sticky Whirls there, as well," added Meg, handing out another threepence with the desperate prodigality demanded by the situation.

"O.K. So long's I needn't take Peter."

Evidently Johnnie had divined that he was in a strong bargaining position. He still hovered on the caravan steps.

"Will Mummy have stopped crying in time for the bathe?"

"Yes, of course. That is, Mummy's not crying, she's only got a headache," Meg amended, loyal to the fiction by which Isabel was trying to sustain her self-respect.

"Her headache, then," agreed Johnnie amiably, though a trifle impatient at such irrelevancies. "Will it have stopped in time for the bathe?"

"I expect so——we'll see. Run off quickly, now, or Peter will be back from the Hutchinses and then you *will* have to take him."

Johnnie thus disposed of for half an hour or so, Meg turned back to her sister.

"Now, then," she resumed. "Start at the beginning. It's something to do with Philip, isn't it?" she hazarded.

"So you guessed? You noticed the likeness, too?"

"Guessed what? What likeness? What are you talking about, Isabel?"

"Oh! Oh, I'm so ashamed, now, ever to have thought of such a thing!" Isabel buried her face in the cushions so that her next words were almost inaudible. "But I suppose you'd better know—now that Philip himself knows, I mean. Oh, Meg, I've been imagining—for days—ever since I sent you that telegram—I've been imagining that perhaps Philip *was* Uncle Paul!"

It was a bewildering story, as told by Isabel to an accompaniment of sobs and sniffs, her face half smothered in the cushions, and with the people in the next caravan playing "Everybody loves a Fat Man" on their gramophone.

But gradually Meg came to understand it. How Isabel had married Philip after an extremely short acquaintance, and knowing next to nothing about him; how, right from the start, although she had been fascinated by him, charmed by his air of strength and experience, she had also been afraid of him, afraid of his reserve; of his cold, censorious manner; afraid above all of her own ineptitude when it came to dealing with the inevitable difficulties of his relationship with his stepsons. And in the face of her fears and lack of self-confidence, Philip also had grown uneasy; and his uneasiness had shown itself not in greater tolerance towards his new family, but in greater coldness and withdrawal. His moments of tenderness and unreserve with Isabel had grown rarer, and his difficulty in adjusting himself to the company of two small boys had increased.

Isabel's blundering attempts to defend him against their tiresomeness, and to defend them against his half irritable, half conscientious attempts at discipline, had only made matters worse. And then had come this disastrous caravan holiday, culminating in Mildred's dramatic resurrection of the ghost of Uncle Paul.

Isabel, always easily influenced, had from the first taken Mildred's fears with great seriousness. She had looked round among their acquaintances for possible Uncle Pauls, making all allowance for fifteen years of change, and for possible disguise. She had looked, at first, solely on Mildred's behalf; and she could not tell, now, exactly when it was that she began to be afraid not for Mildred, but for herself.

For, of all their acquaintances, was not her own husband the man who most nearly fitted the rôle? Of his past life she knew nothing, apart from his own assertion that it had been spent in the army, mostly abroad. His appearance fitted well enough. He was dark, not very tall, and though he seemed a much broader, more thick-set man than she remembered Uncle Paul to have been, that was a change only to be expected in the development from youth to middle-age. He claimed to be fifty-two—a good deal older than Uncle Paul would have been—but who could say if this was his real age? With his upright carriage and brisk manner he could easily have been forty-five or less—and anyway, mightn't Uncle Paul have aged far beyond his years during his time in prison?

Just what Meg herself had been wondering about Freddy, only in reverse. The soul-destroying life of prison ages a man. The sheltered life of prison preserves a man's youth. Was one guess as likely as the other?

Isabel was continuing:

"But the chief thing, Meg, was that he somehow gave me the same sort of feeling. The way he glances up in a quick, absorbed sort of way from something he's doing. The graceful definite sort of way he moves across a room. Oh, I don't know! Once I began thinking about it, there seemed to be hundreds of little things! Oh, Meg, you've no notion how easy it is, once you get an idea like that into your head, to fancy you're seeing evidence for it everywhere! I realise now, of course, what it must have been. As a child I was half in love with Uncle Paul—I suppose we both were—and if you're in love with a man, I think the feelings you have about his way of moving and everything are the same as the feelings you'd get about any other man you were in love with. It's in *you*, I mean, really, more than in him. And so you see all kinds of likenesses that aren't really there, if you see what I mean . . ."

Meg's thoughts were wandering up a sudden byway of hope. Could she, too, be imagining a likeness that wasn't there, and for the same reason? Could Freddy's volatile charm be not so much like Uncle Paul as like Meg's image of an ideal lover . . . ?

But for the moment she must listen to Isabel, who was still recounting the evidence which, it had seemed to her, was piling up against her husband. Such as the fact that he seemed to have no family or close friends. Of course, it was natural enough that a man turned fifty, an only son, should not have many relatives still living; and equally natural that a man who had spent most of his adult life abroad should have had little chance to make friends in his own country. The circumstances were easily explicable, but all the same they were unfortunate in view of the turn his wife's thoughts had begun to take.

"You could easily have checked up on his army career, I should have thought," remarked Meg at this point. "You could have asked at the War Office—they keep records of everything. I expect they could have told you exactly how many pairs of boots he's had in the last twenty-five years, and in which parts of the world, and how much they cost."

"I know," said Isabel helplessly. "But it seemed such an awful thing to think of doing. Besides, I wouldn't know how to go to the War Office. Don't they have a sentry outside, or something? I wouldn't know what to say, or what to wear, or anything."

For a moment Meg was shocked. Isabel had, indeed, played the part of a loyal wife in all this; but had her loyalty rested on no securer foundation than diffidence—on sheer, silly incompetence?

But it was wrong to be shocked. Who has ever been able to analyse the motives, good and bad, large and petty, heroic and ludicrous, which add up to such qualities as loyalty and courage? Isn't it enough that they do add up?

Or don't. Meg's own situation loomed terribly before her for a moment. Then she fastened her attention again on Isabel's confession.

". . . And all the time I kept having to go up to the cottage to see Mildred . . . And that kept reminding me of things. Things I'd heard and quite forgotten. How Uncle Paul had once tried to trip Mildred up into the well one dark night—he'd put a barrow across the path so that she'd have to go round . . ."

Isabel did not seem to notice Meg's sudden movement; her voice went on, and by the time Meg was properly attending again she had come to quite a different subject.

"Philip was so nice about it!" she was saying. "You can't imagine! Most men would have been furious—would have hated and despised a wife for suspecting such things. But he—well, this seems to be the kind of thing he *does* know how to be nice about. It's the *little* things that make him angry, not big ones at all. Oh, Meg, he's so good! You know, you can't ever really understand a man until you've thought he's a murderer!" Isabel raised her face from the cushions with a look of quite ridiculous bliss. "Until I began wondering if Philip was Uncle Paul, I'd never really *thought* about him, if you know what I mean. But this made me really look at him—wonder about him—try to understand what went on in his mind. It was fright that made me do it, but after a bit I found that the things I was discovering weren't frightening at all. This sounds quite idiotic—but it was thinking he was a murderer that made me notice for the first time how completely reliable he is. Do you remember that time when he'd taken Johnnie out sailing, and I was so scared they were going to rub each other up the wrong way? And you said—I forget what exactly, but anyway it made me realise all of a sudden how extraordinary it was that, suspecting what I did, I should still only be worrying about them having a row, and not a bit about the possibility that Johnnie might be in danger. That's when I first noticed that in spite of everything, in spite of all my suspicions, I still *knew* that he would take care of Johnnie.

"That made me try and work it out. I began to notice that I was only *really* frightened of Philip being a murderer at the times when he wasn't there. When he was away in town—that sort of thing. Each time, I was terrified of him coming back; and each time when he did come back, somehow it didn't seem so bad. It seemed—Oh, I know it all sounds very contradictory, but this is how I felt—it seemed that the more frightened I was about him being Uncle Paul, the less frightened I was about everything else. His sharp strict ways weren't terrifying me as they used to. On the contrary, they were making me feel safe."

"I think they've been making the boys feel safe all along," remarked Meg. "I always thought that when he scolded them it was *you* who were upset—not them at all."

"I know—I know that now. But I was frightened of him, you see. I thought he was dreadfully strict and short-tempered. So he is, of course, but I feel now that that's all part of what makes him such a good person to lean on. I like it. It's what I need. It's a funny thing, you know, Meg," she finished dreamily, "you find in the end that you've married a man because of all the qualities you thought you were marrying him in spite of."

With this profound though ungrammatical reflection, Isabel relapsed into smiling silence. It seemed a pity to disturb so blissful a state, but Meg had to ask one more question.

"By the way," she said. "How *did* you find out for certain that he wasn't Uncle Paul?"

"Oh. Oh yes, well, that was just a coincidence, really. It's funny how unimportant it seems now. You know Mrs Hutchins who keeps popping in, and her husband used to be in the army? Well, what with Philip being away so much, and Mr Hutchins spending so much time asleep with the *Daily Mirror* over his face, they'd never really met. And then, this morning, they happened to run into each other by the tap. Mr Hutchins recognised Philip at once—apparently he'd served under him in Egypt, or somewhere, ten or twelve years ago. I found them reminiscing, each with an empty jug in his hand, when I went to see what had happened to the water. So of course I knew, then, that if Philip had been this man's commanding officer for three years quite soon after Uncle Paul was sentenced, then he couldn't possibly be Uncle Paul, could he?"

Again Meg was shocked. It seemed a precarious sort of faith in one's husband that could be restored so completely by so fortuitous a circumstance. Yet who, again, has the right to criticise the foundations of another's faith? If Isabel lacked strength, then what could she do but use the qualities that she did possess? With only weakness, diffidence and suggestibility to aid her, she had still won though. Wasn't this a special kind of courage of its own?

And she had been honest, too, in her muddled way, to both Philip and herself.

"So there was no need, really, ever to have told Philip about your suspicions?" Meg observed, at the end of her reflections.

Isabel looked vague.

"Well—no—I suppose there wasn't, really. But I was crying, you see, and feeling so fond of him, I just couldn't help it. And he was so nice. You wouldn't think, would you, that anyone with such a logical mind could be so understanding," she added, with unconscious paradox.

Silence fell again. When Isabel spoke again it was on so different a topic that for a moment Meg was at a loss.

"You know it's the seventh of August tomorrow?" she said; and then, as Meg merely stared, she continued. "Yes—you know. Mildred. The seventh hour of the seventh day. Don't you remember? Not that there's anything in it," she went on hastily. "As you say, it's just Mildred's nonsense. But all the same, you can't help being a little anxious. You know—one does hear of people having things predicted by fortune-tellers, and then the thing happens just because they're expecting it to. Sort of subconsciously making it happen, somehow. Or they die of fright waiting for it. Something like that. That's why we thought it was important for Philip to go up to town and find out about Uncle Paul *today*. So that we can reassure Mildred before the morning. He'll get the news through to us somehow, he says. *He* thinks it's important, too; and nobody could call him superstitious," she concluded, a trifle defensively.

"Well—I agree," said Meg slowly. "I'm sorry if I made light of it before."

She did not mention to Isabel the other possibility that had occurred to her—namely, that some third party might have had a hand in the predictions; might, for some reason of his own, have bribed the fortune-teller to lay stress on this day and hour. Some third party. It seemed better, even in her own mind, to label the person thus, with no name, no identity.

"Yes—and another thing," Isabel was continuing. "I—we—think Mildred shouldn't be left alone too much before Philip gets back with the news. I think you ought to stay with her, Meg, as much as possible. Where is she now?"

"Why—well, actually, I don't know," said Meg. "She was at the hotel this morning, I know, because I phoned and they said——"

She stopped in mid-sentence. *Did* she know that Mildred had been there when she telephoned. All she knew for certain was that an unknown—or at any rate unrecognised—male voice had said that Mildred was there; had said she was having a bath. The last that Meg herself had actually seen of Mildred was last night, before she went to bed. And before her nightmare. Before she found her door bolted on the outside; and before that puzzling silence from Mildred's room. Yes, and before the discovery of the hat box with its stains of blood . . .

But it was no use frightening Isabel.

"I'll go and find her at once," she said; and moved quietly out of the caravan.

CHAPTER XXII

By evening Mildred had still not been found. No one at the Sea View Hotel seemed to remember having seen her today—but then, on a lovely day like this, nearly everyone had been down on the beach. And she was not at the cottage either. This information had been given by Cedric, who had returned from his trip thither barely an hour ago.

In spite of her anxiety, Meg smiled a little as she recalled the humiliating circumstances of Cedric's return. Scarlet, furious, yet still contriving a certain aloof dignity, he had entered the hotel under the irate escort of Miss Carver. "Escort" indeed is something of a euphemism; she was, in fact, pulling him by the ear; and while keeping her relentless grip on him with one hand, with the other she brandished in triumph the lost hat box.

"Taking *my* hat box out of the hall! To put a *snake* in!" Miss Carver could not get over the enormity of it. "Just simply taking it! And look—just look at the stains! They'll never come out—never!"

She displayed the blood-stained lining for all to see, while the unhappy Cedric continued to stumble through his excuses.

"I'm very sorry," he said. "It was Lady Clorinda's steak. I had no idea it would drip so much. That's why I didn't bring your hat box back at once. I'd been going to clean it for you if you'd only waited a bit—"

"Waited! What an idea! For my own hat box!"

"And if you hadn't been in such a hurry," continued Cedric, his own grievances gaining momentum and sweeping away all thoughts of further apology, "if you hadn't been in such a hurry, I wouldn't have lost Lady Clorinda. If only you'd waited till I got back here, instead of insisting on my opening it up on the cliff the minute you met me—"

The altercation had gone on for some time, and had ended with Cedric, humiliated but unbowed, going back to the cliff in the forlorn but unquenchable determination to find his cobra. The pathetic improbability of the success of this enterprise caused Meg to feel, for the first time, a spark of real friendliness towards the provoking lad; and she was quite unreasonably relieved when she saw Captain Cockerill scuttling after him, agog with advice and encouragement.

"You have to sing to them," he was calling out. "A monotonous note—like this—Oo-oo-oo. I've heard the chaps do it in India. I'll come and help you . . ."

Meantime, Miss Carver had settled down in the lounge to air her grievances. The biggest one, really, seemed to be that Cedric should ever have possessed the forty-five shillings necessary to purchase the creature.

"Forty-five shillings! For a boy of twelve! Forty-five shillings to spend on rubbish! Why, when I was his age I thought myself lucky if I had as much as twopence to spend as I liked! There were eight of us, you know, and my dear mother always insisted that any birthday money should go straight into the savings bank. How wise she was!"

Miss Carver gave a self-satisfied sigh as she contemplated the maternal wisdom which had, presumably, saved her vicarage home from being over-run by eight cobras.

"The discipline; the wise and gentle guidance of good parents; that's what the young people lack today—and just look at the result!"

Everyone looked obediently at the hat box; and no one dared to remark that the occurrence was an unusual one, even among young people of today. Only the quiet little lady with the embroidery ventured to remark:

"Well, I don't know. Poor Mrs Forrester. One must be charitable, you know. It must be difficult to bring up a boy without a father."

Miss Carver sniffed. Charitableness had, of course, been inculcated both by Mama and Papa; but it could be misplaced. Was, indeed, almost always misplaced in the case of people one actually knew.

"Rubbish!" she snapped. "A woman can discipline a boy just as well as a man can. In my day, widows were doing it by the thousand, and with most creditable results. And with no help from the Welfare State, either. Whenever I hear that a child is going to the bad because he hasn't got a father, I always ask the same question: *Why* hasn't he got a father? In nine cases out of ten, it's not that the father is dead, it's that he's gone off somewhere. Gone off because his wife doesn't know how to hold him. It stands to reason that the kind of woman who doesn't know how to keep a man contented and under control won't know how to keep a child contented and under control either. To say that a broken home causes a child to go astray is like saying that a broken teapot causes a broken plate. Really it's just that the same housemaid has dropped both of them."

Meg got up and slipped quietly out of the room, out of the hotel. It was no use sitting in there waiting for Mildred to turn up. She might not turn up. And presently it would be dark; and then the difficulties of the search would become grim indeed.

Mildred must be alive. Meg would not allow herself to consider any other possibility; would not plan her search on any other assumption. Yet, as she listed in her mind all the places where Mildred might have been spending the day, she could not visualise them clearly, could not concentrate on them. Another picture got in the way; a picture of weeds, deep and tangled as a dream, where a body could lie hidden as if sunk in deep water: or sunk deeper still in the echoing emptiness of a covered well . . .

The long heat of the day was over, yet still the beach was strewn with people. From up here, on the cliff top, they looked like so much litter left behind by the ebbing tide; and Meg felt a sudden, ridiculous anger that not one of them was Mildred. Surely someone, somewhere, if they only understood how important it was, would have the consideration to be Mildred. Particularly those in yellow dresses . . .

But it was no use wasting her energy and her temper by wandering about in this planless way. One person alone could not scour the neighbourhood before nightfall. Meg sat down on the short grass and tried to examine her situation clearly and reasonably.

It pays to be reasonable, at first. Meg's reasonable thoughts began by leading to the most safe and comfortable conclusions. For what was there alarming, after all, in someone who is on holiday going off somewhere for the day—particularly on a lovely sunny day such as this had been. And hadn't all the unfortunate, and apparently gruesome, little incidents been explained away? The blood-stained hat box had merely contained raw meat from the butcher. The cobra had been put in the cottage by Cedric, who had considered it a convenient hiding place for his unpopular pet.

But why had he considered it a convenient hiding place? Meg lay back on the damp turf, and shading her eyes against the silvery evening light she recalled that important question which she had failed to ask Cedric this morning. What had made him think that it would be possible to keep a snake in the cottage undiscovered? Who had told him that the cottage was empty?

For a careful, calculating boy like Cedric would scarcely have chosen his hiding place at random; impulsively or out of mischief. Had he, then, confided in somebody whom he had reason to suppose would help him? And had that somebody seized the chance and encouraged him—urged him—to keep the cobra in a place where (unknown to Cedric) Meg (or did the person imagine it would be Mildred?) was certain to come upon it?

And if so, had that person known that the cobra had had its fangs drawn? If he had known, then his motive could only have been to frighten the two women—or maybe only one of them—away from the cottage.

But suppose he had *not* known that the creature was harmless? Meg remembered how unwillingly, and under what desperate pressure, Cedric had divulged this shameful fact to her. It was likely, then, that his previous confidant had *not* been told: had imagined that the reptile was deadly dangerous; and, imagining this, had arranged for it to be in Meg's room, waiting for her . . .

But wait. Miss Carver was right. Forty-five shillings *was* a lot of money for a twelve-year-old to have by him. Suppose this unknown person had not merely encouraged Cedric to keep the snake at the cottage, but had actually urged him to buy it—perhaps lent or given him money for this purpose? Someone who already knew that Cedric would like a snake for a pet. Someone who had heard that conversation between Cedric and Captain Cockerill about the taming of snakes. Hadn't they still been discussing it as they came into the lounge that evening after the walk . . . ?

Freddy. Freddy, lounging in the best armchair, his legs stretched out before the luxury of the electric fire. Freddy could have heard it all. Freddy knew all about the cottage; which was Mildred's room, and which was Meg's. And the snake had been in Meg's room.

Police protection. That's what people ask for when they feel they are being threatened. After all, she didn't *know* that it was Freddy. No one in the whole world even knew that she suspected it. If she appealed to the police now, no one could call it treachery to the man she loved.

No one but myself. That's the only person I shall have to face, for all the rest of my life. Myself. The woman who in the face of danger could betray the man she loved.

But do I love him? Perhaps it's not real love; perhaps it's just infatuation. That would make the issue so much easier.

Yes; that's what words like "infatuation" are coined for; to make issues easier. For infatuation is the same as love. Anyone who has experienced it knows that very well, though only a very few dare say so afterwards. For infatuation means "A love that it is inconvenient to go on with." Or disastrous. Or wicked. Never mind, the principle is the same. For one reason or another, it is inexpedient to go on with it, so let us call it by a different name, then the loss will not seem so great. Let us say not "I dropped a five pound note into the fire today," but "I dropped a piece of paper into the fire today." It is just as true, and yet it does not sound like loss at all.

But perhaps I shall *really* stop loving him if I find he's done a thing like this. That's what the girls in the stories do. They find that a man "isn't worthy of their love," and so they stop loving him. Just like that. Like deciding that pineapples aren't worth the three shillings and sixpence they charge for them.

Suddenly Meg felt cold. Perhaps they are right, these stories that I sneer at. Perhaps that is exactly what happens: you simply do find that you no longer love a man after he has done something disgraceful. Perhaps life really is as simple as that. And as paltry—and as disappointing.

So Mildred must have felt, so she must have reasoned, before she dashed off to the police station through that sultry August evening all those years ago. I no longer love him, and so there is no link between us. Where there is no love there can be no betrayal . . .

No love. Meg tried to bring Freddy's face before her mind's eye. Freddy smiling; Freddy with his brows raised in quizzical retort; Freddy happy; Freddy excited; Freddy being gravely absurd. Did the pictures bring the old warmth, the old exciting lurch to her stomach, half laughter and half love?

"Hullo. Is it Babes in the Wood this time?"

Meg opened her eyes. Or was it, perhaps, just one more of the pictures in her mind? Freddy's face, whitely smiling, hung like a moon above her, and for a moment she could focus neither eyes nor thoughts. She stared stupidly. The lurch came to her stomach indeed, but now it seemed to be a mere physical sensation, unrelated to any emotion. She did not even feel frightened. Just puzzled; that was all.

For it had grown dark. While she had been lying here, wondering, quibbling, prevaricating within her own soul, she had allowed it to grow dark; and with the darkness had come Freddy, his eyes as cold and glittering as the stars themselves which were already spread above her in their countless thousands.

No, not cold; wasn't that laughter that glinted in them like sparks of frost? He was laughing at her . . . pulling her to her feet . . .

"Come on," he was saying. "You'll freeze to death. No one's going to cover you with leaves at this time of year, you know."

Not with leaves. With weeds, then; with thick, juicy triumphant weeds, waiting even now in silent battalions . . .

"What *is* the matter?" Freddy was peering closely into her face, his eyes looking huge and brilliant in the starlight. "You're frozen. I'd better take you back."

Meg let him take her arm, and went with him unresistingly.

But back? Back where? Somehow she had assumed that he meant back to the town; back to the lights; back to the companionable crowds. Not back to the cottage . . . backwards . . . forwards . . . into the misty darkness of the cliff top.

She drew away.

"Come on," he repeated. "Mildred's there, you know, she's waiting for you."

"Mildred? She's all right, then? She's alive?"

The words were involuntary; and foolish. If Mildred were waiting, how could she not be alive? Waiting for Meg to join her among the deep weeds? . . . or in the glistening, slimy bottom of that well? . . .

"Of course she's alive! Very much so. In fact, she's just turned me out of the house. So I won't come in with you; I'll just see you safely across the fields."

Freddy's grip on her arm was hard; frightening . . . And yet if he had let go, she knew she would have been more frightened still. As if the hand which she knew and loved had power to protect her from the mind, the purpose, which as yet she did not know . . .

For he could be lying. Mildred might not be there at all. When they got there, the cottage might be empty and silent. She could be alone there, beyond reach of help; alone with Freddy—or would he, by then, be Uncle Paul?

Suddenly she knew what she must do; and with the knowledge came a strange, exhilarating sense of victory; though whether it was the victory of triumphant love or of sheer hysterical terror she could not yet tell.

"Freddy," she said. "Are you really Uncle Paul? You look terribly like him."

It was done. The cards were on the table. She was no longer deceiving him, no longer holding any advantage over him. He had been warned, but not betrayed. Anything he did now, anything he forced her to do, he would be doing with his eyes open.

And in return for all this she had naturally expected that something decisive would happen. That he would turn and strangle her then and there? That he would somehow instantaneously prove his innocence? She waited, tense, exultant, and the pale smudge of his face seemed to twist and flicker in the starlight.

"Good lord!" he said, after a short silence. "You girls do know how to make the most of a humdrum seaside holiday, don't you?" And then, after another pause: "I'm flattered. You were in love with the bloke, weren't you?"

"Yes. In a way." Meg felt strangely at ease in this bizarre conversation. "I was. As much as you can be at six years old. And you're terribly like him. So I wondered. And I thought I'd better simply ask you."

"It's not unknown, you know," said Freddy slowly, "for a girl to fall in love with the same type of man every time. That's why I'm flattered, of course. But look here"—he spoke more briskly—"what can I say? If I *was* this Uncle Paul of yours, then obviously I'd say I wasn't. But—let's be fair—if I *wasn't* him, it would still be reasonable to say that I wasn't, wouldn't it? So there's really no way I can set your mind at rest. Now, is there?"

"I—I suppose not," said Meg weakly. "But—but if you could just tell me some of the things that have puzzled me. Like why you came down here at all. And how you come to be staying at the same hotel as Mildred."

"Why I came here? Because you did, of course. I thought it would be rather fun, and I happened to be out of a job. Not such a fearful coincidence really, because I'm more often out of a job than in one. The income which you see me living beyond is a sadly irregular one. And as to Mildred's hotel—well, it just simply happened that it was the only one in the town with any vacant rooms. As you found yourself. They'd had quite a large party cancel suddenly, on the very day when you and I were both room-hunting. Satisfied? I suppose not. Uncle Paul could easily have made all that up. Or it could even have happened to him: murderers have to spend the night somewhere, just like anyone else. I really don't see what I can say to make you believe me."

"Just say you're not Uncle Paul!" cried Meg desperately. "I know you might be lying, but all the same, say it! I know I'd believe you if you did. Say it! Say it!"

"By all means. I'm not Uncle Paul. You see? It doesn't sound a bit convincing. And, unfortunately, I have no family, or relations of any kind, to vouch for me. I'm a Norphan. Brought up in various kind homes and schools. Just the kind of fellow to go to the bad."

"I thought you said you had a sister," interposed Meg quickly. "The one with the studio and the scrambled eggs. You told me. And that you'd quarrelled with her."

"Did I? Well, I must have been lying, I suppose," said Freddy regretfully. "That's what makes it so awkward. I do tell lies." He said it as one might say "I have a weak heart." "But," he added, more hopefully, "if I *had* had a sister I *would* have quarrelled with her. Really I would."

Meg laughed; a sort of clipped, one-syllable laugh, thin and ridiculous under the stars. They walked on a little in silence. Then Freddy said, a little querulously:

"You're being very trusting, Meg, walking along with me like this. Why don't you run away screaming?"

"I don't know," said Meg truthfully. "And I'm not exactly being trusting, you know. It's just that I feel safer holding your arm even when I *don't* trust you." She laughed again, tremulously. "It's silly to feel like that, isn't it?"

"Very silly. Plumb crazy, in fact. But very nice, too. *Very* nice."

Freddy's grip on her arm tightened; he quickened his pace; and now the wet resilience of grassland was past, and their feet were crunching over cinders. Another minute, and the silken visibility of night time suddenly became impenetrable blackness against a shaft of light. They had arrived.

"So Mildred *is* there," said Meg, blinking at the lighted window. "I thought perhaps—"

"I know you thought perhaps," said Freddy brusquely. "But you needn't think it any longer, because I'm taking myself off right now. The big Perhaps is showing a clean pair of heels. And don't press me to stay—you aren't, I notice—but don't, anyway, because the sight of me seems to throw our Mildred into fits. I suppose she thinks I'm Uncle Paul too? You'll be able to have a lovely gossip about it, won't you, all girls together."

Abruptly he dropped Meg's arm, and turned away into the darkness; while Meg, stupefied by doubt, stumbled on, like a moth, towards the light. Through the gate . . . along the garden path . . . and when she bumped up against the wheelbarrow it scarcely registered on her mind at all. So little, indeed, that it might, after all, have been chance rather than caution which made her scramble past it on the side away from the well.

CHAPTER XXIII

Meg had not expected to sleep that night. She had come to the cottage tense and frightened, spurred on by a sense of climax; a mounting dread for herself; for Mildred; for them all.

She had stopped wondering if her fears were reasonable; she did not even know whether she was astonished or only relieved to find that Mildred was indeed waiting at the cottage, the lamp lit, and everything apparently in order. Lying now in the great bed, midnight at hand, Meg recalled that her half-sister's demeanour had been calmer, more reasonable, than it had been for days.

Not that Mildred had explained any of the things that had been puzzling Meg. She did not say where she had been all day; nor why, on this night of all nights, she should have come once more to the cottage. Perhaps she had taken it for granted that Meg would be there with her; or perhaps, now that the seventh hour of the seventh day had drawn so near, its fantastic terrors had begun to dwindle, as terrors, even not fantastic ones, are apt to do once they are close at hand.

Nor had Mildred thrown much light on the events of last night. She did not explain how she had managed to sleep through Meg's screams; why she had left so early, and without a word, in the morning.

She had explained nothing; but, on the other hand, Meg had not asked her much. Whether it was simply that her brain was worn out with puzzling about it all; or whether she had, half consciously, already become aware that all these questions were now irrelevant and that the die was already cast; whatever the reason, the fact remained that Meg felt that evening that she just couldn't be bothered with any of it any more. Mildred was found; she was apparently safe and well. Freddy had denied that he was Uncle Paul. And Philip was finding out the real facts. Any minute now, they might get a message. Except, of course, that Philip would be expecting Mildred to be at the hotel, not here; that might delay things a little. But anyway, after seven tomorrow morning the whole silly business would be over. There was just one more night to get through; that was all. One more night.

Against all her expectations, Meg fell asleep.

She woke to find that the first grey glimmer of dawn was already shaping the square of the window. She felt an extraordinary upsurge of triumph. The night was over! This last, dreaded night of climax, of nameless doom—it was already finished—it had been got through. The climax had fizzled out. Meg felt exultant—victorious—as if it was by her own exertion that the hours of darkness had been made to pass; that it was her skill, her persistence, that had brought to birth the day.

She lay for a few minutes drinking in the comfort of her blankets; the security, the reassurance of the growing light. Soon the birds would be singing. Soon the first long shafts of the sunrise would be striking across the untamed leaves of the garden. Soon an occasional car would sound, humming singly through the distance; early labourers would be tramping off to work; there would be a smell of frying bacon. The day would be here.

And Mildred would sleep on. Sleep on, no doubt, through all the growing stir of the morning. Till eight—till nine. Till the sun was high, and all the world was a-bustle. Till the seventh hour was gone—lost for ever in the humming, rattling busy-ness of one more August day.

But as yet, of course, there was only a glimmering greyness; only enough to show up the walls, the furniture, as dim, shapeless mounds. And as yet the birds were not singing; outside there was still a grey, dewy silence, quieter even than the night.

There was a knock on Meg's door.

"Who is it?"

Meg had started up, her bare shoulders shivering in the damp chill of dawn. "Who is it?"

The door opened a little, and it was Mildred peering round. She looked wispy, defenceless, after the night. Her voice was husky, still rasped with sleep.

"Are you awake, Meg? I can't sleep—I think I'll get up and make some breakfast. I thought perhaps you'd like some too."

"Why—yes—I think I would." Meg was rubbing her eyes, unsure. "It's funny—I was awake too. It must be something in the air. I don't think I'll be able to sleep any more."

She put her legs over the side of the bed, and for a minute sat there, stiff, half-dreaming, in this almost unknown hour. Then, slowly, she began to dress, groping for the shadowy shapes of the garments on the chair. She did not want to light a candle. The scrape of the match, the sudden darting dazzle of the flame, would seem out of place, would jar upon the dim coming of the day. Might, it almost seemed, arrest the dawn in its tracks, bring back the darkness. A step back, where Meg knew that she must step forward. Forward, it was the only way; there was no alternative now. The time when she could have stepped back was over . . .

What was she thinking about? What silly, dreamy notions can come into your mind at this strange hour, not yet quite real, with the night not yet quite gone.

Her feet sounded heavy, clashing like great slabs of wood in the silence as she made her way down to the kitchen.

Mildred was already there, fully dressed, and she had managed for the first time to get the rusty, unreliable little oil cooker alight; its flaring, smoky flame was already settling to a steady blue. The smell of paraffin was over-powering, but not unpleasant; it was a warm sort of smell, heralding food, companionship and light.

"I'm making some tea," said Mildred, her voice clear and vigorous now, all huskiness gone. "Go in the front room and I'll bring it to you."

"I'm to be waited on, am I? How nice!" Meg moved through into the other room, where the stove was already opened up and blazing cheerily. Meg shivered a little, not with cold, but with the stiffness, the tremulousness, of very early waking. She sat down near to the inviting blaze, yawned, and gave herself up to watching the firelight as it flickered, brightened and faded on the plastered walls, and the room grew sallow with the coming day.

And now Mildred was here, pulling out the gate-legged table, spreading it with a gay gingham cloth that Meg had not seen before. As she leaned forward into the rosy firelight Mildred's face looked young and soft, her just-applied lipstick shone with dewy freshness.

"It feels funny, all this bustling about at crack of dawn," remarked Meg, smiling, shuddering, and stretching out her feet to the fire. "As if I was catching a train, you know—starting out on some long journey."

Mildred put down the hot water jug with a little thud, and wiped her hands.

"Starting out on some long journey?" she repeated, as if the words were somehow too hard for her to understand.

"Why—yes—I think it feels just like that," said Meg, yawning and shivering again. "Don't you feel it, too?"

Mildred stared at her for a moment in silence. Then at last, unwillingly, and as if strangely disturbed, she answered: "Yes. It's funny—but—I do."

Now here were the two steaming cups of tea. Mildred set them on the table, and sat down opposite Meg, sipping her own tea and watching Meg in a silence that had somehow, imperceptibly, grown uneasy.

"Is it too hot?" she asked suddenly, seeing Meg set her cup down after a single sip. "Isn't it as you like it?"

"It is a bit hot," admitted Meg. "And, actually, Mildred, you know, I don't take sugar."

"Don't take sugar? Oh, but you should, you know, so early in the morning. It wakes you up. It gives you energy. Drink it up and you'll see."

Obediently Meg sipped some more of the tea. After Mildred's unwonted kindness in getting the fires going and making the tea for them both, Meg did not like to hurt her feelings.

But the tea was really sickly sweet: it was impossible. Meg could only manage a few mouthfuls. She waited till Mildred had finished hers, and then jumped up and hustled the two cups together into the washing-up bowl, hoping that Mildred had not noticed how much she had left.

Mildred was making porridge now. Leaning over the heavy, over-large saucepan, stirring earnestly, her face creased with the anxiety of the inexperienced cook. Stirring, stirring, as if she would never end.

And then, suddenly, she stopped stirring. The dull tap of the spoon against old iron ceased; and Mildred, her head raised, her whole body poised, seemed to arrest the very movement of the air with the intentness of her listening.

But Meg could hear nothing. Nothing within the cottage or without, except the all-enveloping murmur of the brightening day.

The moment relaxed. The stirring continued. But Meg could now no longer forget that the seventh hour must be coming very close. What time was it? Half past five? Six? Already, while her back had been turned, the wet, glittering pinkness of the air had brightened, and the little dusty windows were damp with the morning.

Meg tired of watching the stirring. It was making her drowsy again; it seemed to go on and on. She wandered back into the front room to set the table. A spoon each. Sugar. More cups. There wasn't much you needed to lay for a breakfast of porridge.

And now here was the porridge, steaming hot, and not lumpy at all. Mildred had done well.

But—oh dear!—this time, how salty it was! Mildred was certainly overdoing her flavourings this morning—or was it Meg who was being hypersensitive? She forced herself to eat a few spoonfuls, and then, in a moment when Mildred had gone back to the kitchen for more milk, she slipped to the door, opened it, and flung most of what was left into the kindly oblivion of the weeds.

"Why have you opened that door?"

Meg had only just managed to slip back into her place, and set the almost empty plate in front of her, when Mildred returned from the kitchen. She looked startled rather than accusing.

"I thought it would be nice to have some fresh air," said Meg. "It's a lovely morning. Look. The sun's coming up."

It was. From where she stood, Mildred stared out through the doorway into the glancing crimson light. But the light of sunrise was harsh to her carefully made-up face. The rouge which had looked so soft and bright by firelight was now hard and ageing; the cheeks sagged a little beneath it, and the thick pinkish powder seemed only to throw into relief the lines running from her eyes and across her forehead. Almost as if she knew all this, Mildred sat down abruptly in her place, ducking away from the cruel and lovely light, and began to eat her porridge.

But she ate slowly. Every minute, now, she raised her head to listen; to listen, and to stare at Meg with an intent, half questioning look, which Meg found strangely disconcerting. Uncomfortably, she toyed with the sad remains of her porridge, trying to keep up the pretence of enjoying it.

Neither spoke. Meg was conscious of an uncomfortable beating of her own heart now. What was the time? Half past six? Even a quarter to seven? It was nonsense, of course, all nonsense. Nothing would happen when it was seven.

Why was she so sure it was nonsense? If only her heart would stop beating so loud, she would be able to remember why she was so sure . . .

Through the doorway the misty light was brightening. Its chilly swirls were coiling into the room, sliding along the floor, among the chairs . . . all around her feet, inducing a curious numbness . . . Above the mist, the first great shafts of gold were already slanting towards the doorway. Yet somehow, to the two motionless people within, it was as if not the sunrise, but some vast and devastating fire, was sweeping silently towards them.

There was something wrong. Meg roused herself, looked across the table at her companion. Why, Mildred must be ill! She was swaying in her seat . . . lurching from side to side . . . she must be fainting . . .

Yet as Meg moved to go to her aid, the strange thing was that the table began swaying too, as well as Mildred . . . and the walls . . . and the floor . . . There was a sudden clatter of a spoon, and Meg saw that it was her own spoon that had slipped unfelt from her hand.

She stumbled, clutched the table, and regained her seat again. Her movements, startling and perilous as they had seemed to her, must in reality have been slight, for Mildred seemed to have noticed nothing. She was listening again: her eyes fixed on the brightness of the open door. Meg controlled her faintness. It must be the result of getting up so early, and then all this nervous strain. They must both pull themselves together. If only Mildred would speak, would break this tense and expectant silence.

And then Mildred did speak.

"Die!" she screamed to Meg across the bright little breakfast table. "Why don't you die?"

And then her swaying, wavering figure seemed to be rising up, looming giant-wise towards the ceiling. Her voice came down to Meg huge as a voice from heaven, yet hoarse with fury.

"Why don't you die?" it roared again. "There was enough in that tea—that porridge—to lay out ten men! Why don't you die?"

Meg was aware of a hand shaking her, of the voice going on and on, louder and louder in her ears.

"It was *you* who made me betray him! You, with your nosy, precocious, interfering ways! If it hadn't been for you I'd never have seen that newspaper—never have known the danger! If it hadn't been for you I'd never have been out of my mind with shock so that I rushed for the police! If I hadn't betrayed him he'd have loved me—he *did* love me! He'd planned to kill me, but he loved me too, I know he did! If only I'd stuck by him—if only I'd braved everything, risked everything . . . ! And it was *you* who prevented me— *you,* you sneaking, scaremongering little tell-tale—you bossy, nosy, interfering little brat!" Mildred's voice sounded hollow now, and trembling, like some strange and terrible instrument: "And now you're trying to interfere again . . . trying to be here when he comes . . . to let him find *you* here waiting . . . you, looking just as I looked once . . . You, with all the youth and freshness that once was mine! Was that why you dressed up in my clothes? The clothes I was wearing when he came through this very door . . . one summer morning . . . and I was setting his breakfast on this very table, and he took me in his arms and told me I looked lovelier than the rising sun . . ."

Mildred's voice had grown soft, and Meg could scarcely hear the words. Now it rose again to a harsh scream.

"He's coming! He's coming! But he shan't find you here, he shan't! Die! Die quickly before he comes!"

Meg did not know if it was a blow from Mildred's hand that struck her to the ground, or if it was only her own throbbing, overpowering dizziness. Whichever it was, it was strange that there should be such a sudden silence. Was it always silent like this down here among the chair legs and the old warped boards? Or was Meg growing deaf as the drug forced her ever nearer to oblivion?

No: it must be that Mildred's voice had indeed ceased; ceased abruptly; silenced by a sudden terrible fear—a sudden terrible hope.

For far away along the track came the crunch-crunch of distant feet.

Mildred had leaped to the doorway, her face lifted, as in worship, towards the rising sun.

"Die! Die!" she screamed again—but now her voice seemed raised less in threat than in frantic, ancient prayer. "Die! He shan't find you here, he shan't! Whether he comes for love or for revenge, he comes to me—to me alone!"

The huge golden light of morning was upon her. For a second Mildred stood poised, as if facing as an equal the glory of the rising sun; and then she began to run. To run and run towards the gate, towards the blinding brilliance of the sunrise. And the rising light swept over her like a tide, filling her eyes, her soul, buffeting her with silent waves of gold, until, perhaps, she scarcely knew that it was the wooden handle of a barrow, not sunlight, that struck her thigh; and as she veered sideways, towards the well, towards the final, fatal crash, she may have fancied that she was still plunging, dazzled by the glory of the morning, towards her murderer, her love.

And so she never knew that the footsteps on the cinder track were only those of Philip and a young policeman, bringing with them the news that Paul Hartman had died in prison four years ago.

CHAPTER XXIV

They thought that Meg was still unconscious; and indeed she still could not bring herself to move or open her eyes. But at intervals she could hear their talk quite clearly; could understand clearly too, perhaps more clearly than ever before.

It was understanding that they were talking about at this very moment. Isabel's voice, pitched low but quite distinct:

"The funny thing is, Meg is the one who will understand, better than any of us, why she did it. They were so alike, you see, though I don't think either of them ever realised it."

But one of them realised it now. Meg's eyes were still closed, but perhaps she could see all the more clearly for that. Could look back over fifteen years, and see a young, romantic girl, so like herself, defiantly setting up idealistic and impractical standards of love and loyalty—and failing to live up to them. Never mind that Mildred's failure was, by most people's standards, unavoidable; that in sending for the police she had only been acting sensibly.

Sensibly. A wild, romantic spirit, believing the world well lost for love—and when the test comes, it finds itself acting sensibly. Sensibly, and with nothing at all to distinguish it from any of the millions of ordinary, timid spirits that pick their way so cautiously through their secure and lukewarm lives.

Meg could feel, as if it was her own, the cruel shock of Mildred's self-realisation all those years ago. The discovery that great, quixotic flights of courage were not, after all, for her.

But only just not. That must have been the bitterest thought of all. When high courage has not been quite high enough; when it has missed heroism by the merest hair's breadth, and yet in its result seems identical with the most craven cowardice—that is the hardest memory to bear.

For fifteen years this had been Mildred's memory. Fifteen years of trying to blur the issue to herself by self-pity, by self-dramatisation, by telling and retelling the story from every false and flattering angle. By marrying, without love, a wealthy man who could fill her life with the sort of pleasures which demand neither love nor loyalty; a life in which self-sacrifice is superfluous, heroism positively farcical.

For a time Mildred had managed to forget.

But fifteen years pass. Paul's sentence will have expired. He may be coming back! He *will* be coming back! And when he comes back he will look for her. He will look for her at the cottage.

For revenge? For love? This time she will risk everything. Without fear she will lay her life before him, and if he should strangle her in the next minute it will still be worth it. This time, she will not fail. This time, for good or evil, she will be on his side for ever.

So much for heroic resolutions. And it is easy to rent the cottage again. But, once there, it is lonely and frightening.

Revenge is a very terrible word to have in your mind day and night . . . especially at night, when unknown footsteps bring terrible fears and hopes . . . and then pass on. It is easier if you talk about it sometimes—to Isabel—to anyone who will listen.

Easier, yes; but it is not wise. For now a fuss is starting; Meg had been sent for . . . everyone is trying to make her leave the cottage . . . and she dare not explain to them why she wants to stay . . .

But the cottage is not only frightening; it is uncomfortable too. Discomforts that were nothing in youth are dreadful now . . . Mildred finds herself for ever seeking excuses to escape them . . . to slip back to the comforts of the town. Fifteen years of idleness and soft living have left their mark for ever.

For ever? Really for ever? Mildred is face to face, like many a woman before her, with the terrible realisation that the attributes of her youth are gone. For years a woman may tell herself that she is still at heart the same lively, courageous, generous girl that she always was. It is merely that, just at this moment, she is too depressed to be lively; too ill-used to be generous; and prudence, not courage, happens to be appropriate on this particular occasion. And then, one day, she wakes up and knows that these feelings, these qualities, are not merely in abeyance, but gone for ever.

Gone for ever are Mildred's looks as well. She can see it. Those discontented lines . . . those sagging cheeks . . . Frantic visits to beauty parlour and hairdresser, the panic purchase of over-young clothes—Mildred knows in her heart that they achieve nothing. What will Paul think of the face, the figure, that he will find at the cottage now?

But he will find Meg's face, Meg's figure. Meg coming in out of the rain, as Mildred once did, rosy and sparkling, and with no need of the bottles and jars that now litter Mildred's room. Meg hanging her shabby raincoat on the very hook where Mildred once hung hers: when hers, too, was shabby, and it didn't matter because the body within was young and firm and shapely beyond the art of any dress designer.

Meg's voice is like Mildred's too, as it used to be; her movements—her hair—she will seem to Paul to be the very girl he left behind, while Mildred will be a middle-aged stranger, of no account.

And Meg *will* be there when he comes to the cottage. There is no escaping it. She is there all day every day now, interfering, impervious. Snubs won't drive her away, nor even threats of danger. In her cocksure, busybody fashion, she thinks she is helping . . . Even as she helped once before . . .

And the cruellest irony of all is that it *does* help. Meg's companionship *does* soften Mildred's fears—the fears that she fights so fiercely to suppress. Meg is courting hatred in the surest way known to human beings—she is pandering to and encouraging the person that Mildred is trying not to be . . .

Suddenly Meg recalled that first morning, leaning over the empty well, with Mildred standing behind her. Mildred, white and shaken with some hidden thought. That was when the idea must have been born. How easy—how very easy!—just a tiny push! Almost an accident, really . . .

But the opportunity passes. Another must be made. For it is becoming urgent now. Paul is coming. He is coming—surely—on the anniversary of his betrayal. The fortune-teller says so. Mildred's own heart says so. Her whole romantic soul flings itself into hope—into belief—into certainty. The date and the hour are fixed irrevocably, by fate and by her own conscience. By that date, by that hour, Meg must be gone.

. . . The obstructing barrow . . . the empty well in the darkness. A trap that could not ensnare Paul himself by accident, for had he not invented it?—and wasn't it already a subtle link between them, that Mildred should adopt it too—a silent uniting of their souls in the solidarity of crime?

Though still it didn't have to be *quite* a crime—it would be Meg's own silly fault if she didn't remember that the well was there. A sort of accident . . . But oh, God, the waiting in that darkened room to see if it happens! The dread that it will . . . that it won't . . . ! And who could have guessed that Meg would have that tiresome boy friend with her, almost as interfering as she is herself?

There was still the snake. Cedric's cobra, that Mildred had helped him to buy. That would be a sort of accident too, of course, for it *mightn't* do any harm . . . and Meg *mightn't* be sleeping at the cottage any more—no one had asked her to. Indeed, they had begged her—warned her—not to do so.

But this plan meant waiting for it to happen, too. Waiting, knowing that there was a snake upstairs. Have other murderers felt this sheer envy of their victims—envy for their ignorance of what is in store? And that very evening Peter had to be playing with Sharkey, making him hiss and squirm, as if deliberately to remind her of the dreadful night to come . . .

The night which *did* come . . . when scream upon scream aroused her . . . Meg's screams. How Mildred must have stopped her ears, buried her head under the bedclothes, praying for it to be finished!

But still it wasn't finished. Here was Meg, alive and well, ringing up the hotel the next morning as if nothing had happened. Mildred could not face the telephone . . . she sent a message that she was having a bath.

And tomorrow is the seventh day. If Meg comes to the cottage tonight, then she must be dead before morning.

And she had come.

Meg awoke from a sort of doze to hear Isabel's voice again:

"It's strange," she was saying. "But I feel, somehow, that it had to happen. I mean the three of us all thinking, in different ways, that Uncle Paul had returned. It was the betrayal, you see, we all felt the guilt of it, I believe, almost as much as Mildred. I know I did—I felt for months—for years— exactly as if I'd done it myself. Of course, I'm rather that sort of person—I do feel guilty about things; but I believe Meg was shocked too—more, perhaps, than she remembers. Because it was she who first found the picture, you know, although she forgot about it afterwards. As if she couldn't bear to remember, I sometimes think . . . Betrayal of a lover—it's a very big thing, when you're young. And so we had to re-live it, somehow, all three of us, each in our own way, and—sort of—try to manage better this time. That's why poor Mildred persuaded herself so completely that he was coming back . . . and I was so ready to believe that Philip might be him . . . and Meg thought that *you* were—"

Now it was Freddy's voice breaking in:

"I suppose she'll know now that I can't be Uncle Paul," he was saying. "But I don't know that I'm a much better bet for her even so. I daresay I *am* like him, as she says. The same type. How much difference do you suppose it makes, Isabel, whether you're actually a criminal, or only the sort of person who easily might have been?"

"I should think it's exactly the same as the difference between a jug that's broken and one that easily might have been," said Isabel. "I mean, one's useless and the other's just as useful as ever. But, of course, I daresay that's just a house-wife's point of view," she added, deprecatingly.

Freddy was speaking again.

"I never had a proper home," he was saying—and his voice was not quite as assured as Meg remembered it—"I never knew my parents, though I believe my father was Italian, or something. They say that boys who've never had a proper home make rotten husbands. Meg may not have heard that—she's very young. Do you think she ought to risk it?"

Meg did not hear Isabel's answer. She wasn't troubled by the thought of the risk, but by the feeling that Freddy sounded different, somehow. Meek—unsure—almost childlike. Under all that flamboyant gaiety, that jesting self-confidence, had there been lurking all the time this hesitant, questioning boy?

But could she love a hesitant, questioning boy? She loved the old Freddy—witty, confident, on top of everything. And he would be like that again—of course he would— when all this upset was over. He would be like that again, and she would still love him, in spite of this glimpse of his weakness.

In spite of it? Suddenly there flashed into Meg's mind the words that Isabel had spoken only yesterday: "It's funny, but in the end you find you've married a man because of all the qualities you thought you were marrying him in spite of."

But she was too sleepy to work it out now. And besides, here was someone else speaking—was it Philip?—saying what a tragedy it was that the news of Paul's death had not reached Mildred in time to prevent it all.

Meg was glad that she still had no strength to speak, and could not answer him. For a strangely vivid picture had come into her mind—a picture of Mildred as she had been in those last minutes before her death, at the triumphant peak of all her wickedness, her silliness, her courage.

For the three were all there, and indissoluble. It might be that some other mind might one day sort them out, might be able to say: "This was courage; this was worth while," and "those were only silliness and wickedness; a dreadful tragedy." But in Meg's eyes they seemed to make a single glittering whole; and as she lay drowsing there, and for long after she had woken, she could feel nothing but gladness that her sister had died as she had, dazzled by the rising sun; died before she could learn that never, now, in either love or hate, would her beloved come striding towards her through the morning.